A
TROUBLED
PEACE

A
TROUBLED
PEACE

L. M. ELLIOTT

KATHERINE TEGEN BOOKS
An Imprint of HarperCollins Publishers

Katherine Tegen Books is an imprint of HarperCollins Publishers.

A Troubled Peace
Copyright © 2009 by L. M. Elliott
All rights reserved. Printed in the United States of America.

Library of Congress Cataloging-in-Publication Data is available.
ISBN 978-0-06-074427-4 (trade bdg.) — ISBN 978-0-06-074428-1 (lib. bdg.)

Typography by Joel Tippie
.09   10   11   12   13   CG/RRDB   10   9   8   7   6   5   4   3   2   1
❖
First Edition

To the memory of my father, who started me on this journey;
And to my guides—my husband, John,
and our children, Megan and Peter—
who have walked it with me.

High Flight

Oh! I have slipped the surly bonds of Earth
And danced the skies on laughter-silvered wings;
Sunward I've climbed, and joined the tumbling mirth
Of sun-split clouds—and done a hundred things
You have not dreamed of—wheeled and soared and swung
High in the sunlit silence. Hov'ring there,
I've chased the shouting wind along, and flung
My eager craft through footless halls of air. . . .

Up, up the long, delirious, burning blue
I've topped the wind-swept heights with easy grace
Where never lark nor ever eagle flew—
And, while with silent lifting mind I've trod
The high untrespassed sanctity of space,
Put out my hand, and touched the face of God.

—John Gillespie Magee, Jr.

CHAPTER ONE

"Pull her up, Henry! Pull her up!"

Henry gripped the plane's steering wheel as it crashed through sun-split clouds toward earth.

He gritted his teeth and waited. Henry had cheated death a dozen times like this during bombing missions over France and Germany. Hurling a plane into a dive to put out an engine fire was the first survival trick pilots learned. They'd earned their manhood during flight training by yanking a plane up just before it smashed into trees or barracks, bragging on how long they'd waited, how close they'd come, how boys who flinched and pulled up early were chicken. Whoever stayed cool longest won bets for three-day passes away from base through such dares. Stupid stuff.

I

Henry couldn't believe he was using the bullyboy tactic, and on Patsy, the person he loved most. But forcing a situation was the only battle strategy Henry knew since going to war. Never second-guess; force a shot-up plane to fly even though ditching was a better idea; charge in with guns blaring; do or die.

"Henry, please. Pull the plane up."

"Not until you say yes. Come on, Pats. *Yes*."

Henry glanced over at Patsy's heart-shaped face. It had that stubborn, I'll-never-admit-to-being-scared look he'd seen countless times on their school playground. He'd always loved what a spitfire she was. But it sure wasn't helping him now.

He calculated the distance to the horizon rushing toward him. He still had a good sixty seconds. He held to his bluff. "I'll pull up when you agree to marry me."

The plane started to buck.

Patsy braced herself. "No, Henry. I love you. But I can't."

"Why not, Pats?"

"I don't think you're ready, Henry."

"Not ready? I spent all my Air Force back pay for the ring. I had a heck of a fight with my dad about buying it. I'd say I'm ready." His voice rattled like the plane. "Please, Pats. Thinking about you, about coming home, is what kept me walking across France, what kept me alive when the Gestapo near drowned me during interrogation. You're my copilot, my navigator. I can't fly straight without you."

For a moment, Patsy wavered. Then she screamed: "Henry—look out!"

Out of the lowering sun swarmed Nazi fighters—Junkers, Messerschmitts.

Twelve-o'clock high—bogeys coming in, fast! Henry heard the voices of his crew shouting, calling out the flight path of the Luftwaffe killers streaking toward them.

Someone radioed American fighters for help: *Little friends, little friends, we've got a hornet's nest here. They're everywhere!*

Do something, Hank. I don't want to die!

BANG-BANG-BANG.

A gray-green Messerschmitt roared past the cockpit, its bullets ripping into Henry's plane, the German pilot's mocking face close enough to see. *Did you really think I would allow you to escape?*

KA-BOOM!

Engines exploded. The plane erupted in a ripple of orange flames. Billowing smoke choked the cockpit. Henry couldn't see anything, couldn't find Patsy anywhere. All he could hear was: *We're cooked, Hank. We're cooked.*

* * *

Henry lurched up, crab-backing into the bed's headboard and banging his skull against his high school diploma hanging above it. He counted the windows—one, two, three. He saw the whitewashed bureau by the door, looked up to see the airplane model he'd made when he was twelve hanging from the ceiling.

Check. Check. Check.

He was in his own bed, in Virginia. Just another nightmare. Another flight into the hell of his own mind.

Kicking back the tangle of covers, Henry fell out of bed and stumbled to his bureau. He picked up a small box and yanked open the starched cotton curtains. Moonlight fell onto his hands as he opened the case. There was the diamond ring Patsy hadn't wanted.

Henry rubbed his face against the ice-cold windowpane to wake himself up completely. He was so sick of his crazy, mixed-up thoughts; these nightmares; the flashbacks to air battles and his struggles on the escape lines of France; the bizarre overlap of his life in Virginia with the memories he was trying to dodge. He was ashamed of knee-jerk reactions like the time Henry's dad, Clayton, shot at a fox in one of the henhouses and the sound of the blast sent Henry bolting across half the county before he recognized he wasn't being hunted himself. It was so hard to know sometimes what was really happening and what was simply his mind playing with him, torturing him just as the Gestapo had set up a fake escape to break his spirit.

He wanted the war in his soul to be over. He was home. Why couldn't he get back to normal? And why wouldn't Patsy marry him?

Henry had set up a perfect proposal, taking Patsy to a dance at Richmond's swank John Marshall Hotel. She'd piled her hair in soft curls and wore a dress she'd borrowed from a society friend she'd met through the Red Cross. It was deep blue velvet with swirls of small beads on its padded shoulders. Very fancy. Very Ginger Rogers. As she held his hand and guided Henry to the dance floor through the mob of returned servicemen and their dates, he knew marrying Patsy was the way back, back to the life he'd planned before the war, before the missions, before all the killing.

As the band played "Till Then," the heart-wrenching song asking the hometown girl to stay true until her soldier returned, Henry held Patsy close and whispered: "Marry me, Patsy." The moment felt like something out of the song, the line he'd hummed over and over to himself in France, *"Till then, let's dream of what there will be."*

But Patsy had said no. Not yet. "You seem so angry," she said, "so haunted. I worry that you think getting married will stop all that somehow. But what if I'm not enough? I don't think I can fix all that. It scares me, Henry." She'd paused, then murmured, "You scare me."

Remembering, Henry butted his head against the glass. *Girl, you don't know scared.* He hadn't told Patsy half of what he'd seen. Boys shredded and blown out of bomb bays to splatter on the glass cockpits of planes following behind in formation. French children so hungry they fought over scraps dropped on the ground by picnicking Nazis. Women dragged out of their homes by neighbors to shave their heads as payback for teenage flirtations with the enemy.

Was he haunted? For sure. Every day in his mind, he walked the hills and streets of France, imagining the fate of those who'd saved him. He reflew his last bombing raid so that Captain Dan lived. He reclimbed the Pyrenees to save his friend, Billy. If only he had been stronger, smarter, done things differently, maybe they'd still be alive. Henry was not quite twenty and already he carried an old man's worth of regret and mourning.

He knew he was jumpy, that his temper had become quick-flint like that of his father, Clayton. He'd tried to explain to Patsy what it had been like—living as a hunted animal behind enemy lines. He had entrusted his life to strangers he couldn't understand, and lived off of adrenaline and suspicion, scrounging for food, scrounging for safety, rarely finding either, day after day, week after week, for months. He couldn't figure out how to shed that kind of battle-ready wariness, that kind of split-second instinct to fight, to run. Half the time, he felt like a lunatic race-horse stuck in a start box. Nobody had said anything in debriefing about how to shrug that off.

Henry covered his face and realized with disgust that his hands were trembling. *You're flak-happy, boy. After all you survived? Now, you start sniveling?* Henry kicked at the heap of blankets, bashed his foot against the bed, and swore loudly.

"Henry, honey? You all right?"

Ma. Henry clapped his hand to his mouth. Poor Lilly had enough to deal with, married to Clayton. She didn't need a basket-case son. Did she know that he got up night after night and walked the lane of their farm to keep from waking her with nightmare screams?

Pulling on forced calm like a flight suit, Henry opened his bedroom door. There stood Lilly, small, sweet-tempered, worried, smelling of talcum powder and the biscuits she'd made for morning. "I'm okay, Ma. Stupid me. Got all tangled up in my covers and fell out of bed just like I used to when I was a kid." He'd gotten so good at faking. Henry tugged the long braid of her graying hair. "Go back to bed, Ma."

Lilly peeped past him to the mess of covers on the floor. "Want me to fix you some hot milk, honey?"

If only warm milk and Lilly's lullabies could settle

him the way they had when he was little. Henry took her gently by the shoulders and walked her back to her bedroom, where Clayton snored. "I'll see you in the morning, Ma."

Henry lingered in the hallway after she closed the door. He didn't want to go back to bed and another nightmare. Instead he dressed and tiptoed downstairs.

Whistling to his dog, Speed, Henry stepped out into the frigid night. He'd walk himself into a dead fatigue. That was the only way he slept sane and quiet.

Chapter Two

Outside the air felt like ice water in his chest. Henry sucked it in, little needles of pain jabbing him awake and clearing his storm-swept mind. He exhaled a thick mist of breath, haloing himself in the moonlight. Behind him his shadow stretched along the frost-slicked grass. Henry smiled. Over in France, on the run with the Resistance, he had hated such clear, starry nights. Back then, his shadow had been a traitorous enemy in bright moonlight, betraying his presence to German sentries. He'd darted from tree to tree to mask his telltale companion, each dash a heart-pounding risk.

But this night on his Tidewater farm, Henry beckoned his shadow as a friend to accompany him and Speed. Once past the chicken houses and into the back fields, he even dared to whistle. Speed trotted along beside him, making all sorts of happy dog noises, snorting and sneezing as he sniffed along the shimmering, crackly ground.

Henry laughed. *See, fool. No Nazis here. Stop being such a birdbrain.*

His whistling turned to humming and then to singing, almost shouting: *"You've got to aaaac-cent-tchu-ate the positive, eeeeee-liminate the negative, latch on to the affirmative, don't mess with Mister In-between . . ."*

Henry tried a few swing shuffles as he sang, imagining the jazzed-up big band sounds of Johnny Mercer's anthem of positive thinking. Speed barked and hopped up and down, nipping at Henry's pants. The two skipped and played, until they tripped over each other and fell into a heap of puppy and boy. Speed slobbered kisses on Henry's face. Henry halfheartedly pushed him away. "Aw, come on, pal, I'm not a kid anymore."

But it was the cold—not decorum—that made Henry jump to his feet. He popped up the fleecy collar of his new flight jacket, to cover his ears. "Darn, Speed. I didn't realize it was this cold again." It'd been wildly warm the week before, hitting ninety degrees one day. While Lilly and Henry happily stood in the sunshine in short sleeves, Clayton had flown into a streak of curses about the fruit trees blooming when it was sure to frost again, killing off their apples.

Clayton was even more cantankerous these days.

Despite the economic boom that had come to Richmond because of war ammunition production and new army facilities, times remained tough for farmers. With gas rationed to just three gallons a week, Clayton couldn't run his tractor and had hitched mules to his plow and wagons. A pair of the obstinate creatures cost him $800—a fortune—and one of them had kicked him good in the leg. Henry figured the only reason Clayton hadn't shot the mule on the spot was the fact that shotgun shells were nearly impossible to buy, rationed along with shoes, tires, butter, and meat.

Using mules had slowed Clayton's work. So had Henry's absence. But Clayton had refused to use German POWs that Camp Peary hired out to local farms and pulp mills. Several Richmond farmers had had most of their peaches ruined when the prisoners picked them well enough but then scratched swastikas into the skin as they packed them for shipping.

Henry had laughed when Clayton had told him that story. He couldn't help it—the gesture of carving swastikas into peaches was so ridiculous. Was that what the war would come to—blind, numb loyalty? In Europe such unquestioning obedience to Hitler would mean a lot more than ruined peaches. It would cost thousands of lives—like the huge casualties in the Battle of the Bulge when the Nazis had stubbornly regrouped in the Ardennes Forest, after being chased across France by Eisenhower's D-day army.

Now Allied leaders were responding to Hitler's unyielding stance with their own brutality, desperate to hasten the war's end. To cripple Hitler's railways and ability to transport supplies and troops, British and American planes bombed cities like Dresden, not just military targets near it. The newspapers weren't real forthcoming about it, but reading in the *Richmond Times-Dispatch* that they'd dropped incendiary bombs filled with phosphorous, Henry knew what "Operation Thunderclap" meant for the civilians down below, the children playing under a war-torn sky.

The firestorm sparked by the phosphorous raged for days across miles of city blocks and created temperatures hot enough to suck people into the flames. The thought of it made Henry want to vomit. God help the crews who had dropped those bombs. Yes, their mission had saved countless American foot soldiers battling their way toward Berlin. But following orders only went so far against the morality of an airman's nightmares once he returned to base and had time to reflect on what he had done.

Henry pushed himself to walk on, marching on a reconnaissance for forgetfulness. Speed silently padded behind him, sensing Henry's tumult, cautious as when Clayton took him on a bird hunt.

But Henry's brooding thoughts kept pace with him.

What about that kind old German sergeant who was supposed to have shot him dead and instead let him go? Would he have shown such pity and generosity to an American boy only to be roasted in an Allied bombing? After her capture, would anyone have been merciful to Madame Gaulloise, the aristocratic woman who got him safely out of Switzerland? And what about Claudette, the beautiful angry Resistant from the Morvan, whose thirst for vengeance would have landed her right in front of retreating Nazi tanks, shaking her fist and harassing them in her rapid-fire French. Would they have just run over her?

The thoughts buzzed around him. He started to run, to flee their attack, but the faces followed, dive-bombing him like Messerschmitts. The image he feared most seeing, couldn't stand thinking about, not knowing, was of Pierre, the solemn little boy who had sheltered him, fed him, taught him, and lost everything—his mother, his grandfather, his farm—because of Henry's presence.

Henry sprinted, stumbling over stones and knee-high meadow grasses, flailing at images only he could see. Henry had left Pierre with a priest when his mother had been dragged away by the French Gestapo, the Milice. Left him with nothing but Henry's good-luck marble. What kind of protection would that be against an enraged, blood-soaked world?

"It's my favorite marble. Mon favori. *I want you to have it.*

That way I'll always be with you. Henri avec Pierre."

"Pour toujours?" *the small boy had whispered.*

"Yes, always. Wherever I go, I remain with you."

Henry fell to his knees, heaving from his run and his guilt about what his escape had cost Pierre, and about leaving him behind. He couldn't have taken Pierre with him, not on the almost suicidal run he'd had to make. He knew that. But was Pierre all right? Had the priest really taken him to a monastery for safety? Had he avoided the Nazi attack on Vassieux that came after Henry fled? Could his mother have survived the Ravensbruck prison the Milice sent her to?

France was in complete upheaval, trying to piece itself back together as Allied forces and retreating Nazis cut a path of destruction across it. Complete victory in Europe was still battles and months away. There was no way to know the answers to any of the questions that hounded him.

Stop thinking! Henry felt as though he was going mad. Patsy was right. He *was* frightening. He frightened himself. He had no idea what memories might grab him by the throat next, or what he might do in response.

God help me. Henry looked up to the stars. Slowly, his panic eased. There, he thought, look how far a soul can stretch. Look at all that black, quiet serenity. Where up there, behind which star did God sit? Could God see the hell on his earth, the barbarity his creations were capable of? Did he weep to see it? How could he not do something to stop it?

No answers came. But out of the darkness of Henry's mind crept the words of "High Flight," a poem that had kept him both grounded and inspired during his combat months, a long-ago faith of his own:

> *"Oh! I have slipped the surly bonds of Earth*
> *And danced the skies on laughter-silvered wings; . . .*
> *Put out my hand, and touched the face of God."*

Henry leaped to his feet. That's right. He could fly. In the sky, he could touch God. Salvation was there.

Henry knew exactly where to find a plane that could take him.

CHAPTER THREE

Old Man Newcomb's place.

Henry lit out across the fields. Newcomb had a Curtiss Jenny, a gorgeous, open-cockpit, WWI biplane—a real gem, since most had been junked long ago. He used it for barnstorming and wing walking. As a boy, Henry had watched Newcomb do daredevil loop-de-loops, whooping and hollering, for the local air circus. The wild-eyed pilot had even taken him up a few times, trying to convince Henry to do wing stunts. It was on those windswept jaunts, in that kite-like machine, that Henry first felt the rush of flight.

In Newcomb's Jenny, he'd leave his nightmares in the dust. It would be real flying, nothing between Henry and the clouds, just a big-ass engine and some fabric-covered wings. No bombs, no flak, no fighters, no worries.

When he saw its brass radiator gleam in the moonlight,

Henry didn't even consider knocking on Newcomb's door. War and living on the run had erased the habit of asking permission. He was going up. Now.

Henry stood on tiptoes to peer at the old-fashioned dial gauges on the control panel. Everything looked fine. He fished around for goggles, finding the long white scarf Newcomb always wore like a flying ace. Like a knight of the skies, thought Henry, as he wrapped it around his throat, his heart filling with the romance, the mystique flying had once had for him.

Then he noticed a tank and a spray boom crammed into the backseat. Newcomb was using the Jenny for crop dusting. Despite his reputation for brewing stump liquor, the old man was getting almost respectable. Last summer, during a polio outbreak, authorities had even trusted Newcomb to fly over the city of Richmond, dumping DDT, an insecticide that killed flies carrying the crippling disease.

But on this night, Henry wasn't interested in respectable. He couldn't stand the idea of anything being dropped out of a plane he was flying. This night was about freedom. This night was about baptism—washing himself clean of death and regrets and disappointment and fear, then beginning life reborn, redefined. This was about the "long, delirious, burning blue . . . the high, untrespassed sanctity of space." Henry heaved the tank out of the plane, laughing wildly when it hit the ground and cracked, releasing a stream of stench.

A jug of moonshine whiskey sat next to the Jenny's wheels. Newcomb was obviously using it to prime the engine. Henry poured the liquid into the engine's little brass cups on the intake manifolds and shut their levers. He rotated the Jenny's thick, wooden propeller five times to suck in the alcohol. Next he'd have to swing the heavy prop hard enough to spark a jump start and pop the engine into running.

Henry threw himself on it. One swing. A cough and sputter.

Another shove. A rattle and die-off.

A third. Nothing at all.

Henry still weighed next to nothing, starved as he'd been on the run in France. He chugged some of the jug's bitter, rancid booze. Feeling it knife through him, Henry hurled his whole being against the prop.

This time it caught and whipped around, nearly whacking Henry as it sped into a whir. The engine spit smoke and the little plane shimmied all over. The delicate cables connecting its two wings hummed, beckoning.

Henry kissed the yellow-painted fuselage, pulled out the wheel chocks, and scrambled into the bucket seat as the Jenny rolled along the grass. He was vaguely aware of Speed barking along behind him, then the sound of another dog howling. He paid no attention.

Henry opened the throttle. He braced his feet against the wooden bar that controlled the tail rudder, wrapped his hands around the long, thin wooden control stick, and pulled.

Bounce, bounce, bounce. The Jenny hopped happily along the ground like a child skipping, so light, so carefree, so different from his B-24, heavy with menace and five-hundred-pound bombs. Each hop lifted the Jenny a little higher for a little longer, until it finally vaulted up over the walnut grove at the field's edge, its wheels brushing the barren treetops with a musical *swish*. Air rushed through the plane's spiderweb of struts and wires, vibrating them like wind chimes.

Henry's soul rang with a long-forgotten joy. He shouted lyrics to a new hit: "I haven't felt like this, my dear, since I can't remember when. It's been a long, long time."

Between that and the steady seep of Newcomb's whiskey into his thinking, it didn't occur to Henry that he was stealing a plane. And he didn't hear the shotgun blasts below.

C'mon, girl. Give me some speed. Henry closed his eyes and held his face up to the winds. *C'mon, a little faster. That's it.*

The Jenny putt-puttered up to its maximum 75 mph, nothing like his B-24's 180 mph, but good enough to smack

Henry's face with a bracing current. He dipped his right wing and skimmed around in a full circle, then tilted left to arc the opposite way in a figure eight, as gracefully as an ice-skater, sliding his way across a vast lake of air.

Henry looked toward the stars that pinpricked the black sky. The Milky Way was so clear, so thick with shimmering lights, it looked like a runway laid out for him. *There, girl.* He pointed. *That'll take us. It's got to be a pathway to heaven. Let's go chase some angels.*

He pushed the throttle's control knob to open it more and pulled back gently on the control stick to tip the plane's nose up into a climb angle. The little Jenny began to tremble. But she dutifully inched higher, about 200 feet per minute.

"I've chased the shouting wind along . . . ," Henry recited. He chortled to himself, his laugh catching in a hiccup of overwrought, tangled emotions—relief, regret, hope.

Come on, sweetheart. Old Man Newcomb said you could reach 6,500 feet. He pulled the stick back a little harder.

The Jenny shook.

Darn it, girl. I'm on a mission, here. Henry's words were slurring. *Don't quit on me now. If I can just get a little higher.*

The Jenny quaked.

C'mon!

The engine belched, gagged, then suddenly silenced.

The Jenny's nose dropped and she began to drift earth-ward, gliding on air. Newcomb did this kind of stunt all the time for the air show. It was like she knew exactly what to do.

For a few long, glorious moments, Henry just grinned and listened to the quiet, waiting to hear a voice—God's voice, any voice of salvation. But when the hum of the struts turned to a shrieking whistle and the wind rushed so fast along his face that it felt like scraping along gravel, Henry realized that he was plummeting. The Jenny could go into a spin. Henry could die.

He didn't care.

It might be better to go this way—quick, in flight, not pulled down and picked apart by his own mind. He sat still a little longer.

Look at that, girl. Dawn's coming. There was the slightest glow of pink along the horizon. He watched it slip along the flat terrain below, tickling the edges of a farm. With the dispassion of a traveler passing through, Henry recognized the layout of his own home.

The Jenny kept falling.

Then a voice did come: *Pull out of this stall, lieutenant. Now, Hank!*

Captain Dan? Henry sat up straight, battle-ready. *Captain, where are you?*

The vision of Dan, wounded, drifting to safety in his

parachute only to be strafed by a Messerschmitt, slapped Henry to attention. *NOOOOOO!* His scream sliced through the silent sky.

Henry grabbed hold of the control stick and pushed forward to regain speed and control of the plane.

The little Jenny bucked, caught some wind, lifted, floated, dipped again, surfaced again. Henry struggled against the flood-water-strong pressure on the foot bar controlling the rudder. The Jenny fishtailed back and forth grotesquely, careening downward toward Clayton's chicken houses. Henry shoved the control stick to bank away, almost flipping the Jenny into a roll. But he righted her and lowered her, and for a few seconds, he had her on the ground, rolling along, soft and smooth.

"Yes, ma'am!" Henry cheered.

But the Jenny had no brakes, and the tailskid wasn't slowing her enough. Henry was fast coming face-to-face with the tree line separating his farm from Patsy's. There was no way to stop. Before he could react, he slammed into it. A wing caught a low-hanging branch; the struts twanged and snapped, and the Jenny tumbled about wildly.

Henry cracked his head against the instruments. The world went black.

CHAPTER FOUR

Henry floated in darkness. His head throbbed with a percussive pounding, like bombs hitting. His ears rang like an air-raid siren. *This can't be heaven. Is it Hell? Just don't let it be another bomb run, please God.*

Henry could make out small, babbling voices. Angels? Devils? The airplane radio? He struggled to hear against the racket in his head.

"Pull off that scarf so I can see his face good. Wait a sec." There was the cold click of guns being cocked and readied.

"All right. Step back quick once you pull it off. There's no telling what this Nazi might do. Six POWs run off two days ago. One of 'em pulled a knife on poor Widow Moore. I about shot that one. Got 'em all rounded up but this one. Beats all. Suppose this stupid Kraut thought he could fly back to Germany?"

Nazis? POWs? Germany? *No, no, no.* Henry couldn't survive another round with the Gestapo. He willed himself to lift his fists, just like Clayton had taught him. *Go down fighting, boy. Don't let them take you easy.*

"Look out! He's coming to."

Two gun barrels rammed up against Henry's chest.

"Hold still, you SOB." A hand jerked the cloth away from Henry's head and bright light hit him like a hammer. Blinking, Henry forced his eyes open.

He heard gasps. The guns pulled back.

"Good Lord!"

"It's Henry Forester!"

"I'll be . . ."

Shielding his eyes against the rising sun, Henry looked around him. He was surrounded by people—the sheriff, Old Man Newcomb, a couple of neighbors, and . . . *oh, no* . . . Clayton. Lilly. And here came Patsy running, trailed by her father carrying his shotgun.

Even with his head thundering, Henry knew. This was no nightmare. This was real.

No one said anything. They waited, dumbfounded. The looks on their faces mortified Henry. Only Lilly's carried pity. Patsy's had the same expression as when she'd turned him down and said he scared her. The moment dragged on and on and on.

Finally, Clayton strode to the cockpit. "Get your butt out of that plane, boy," he ordered.

Clayton offered no helping hand. Henry crawled out and stood shaking, knock-kneed on one of the wings. It was fine. But the other was torn and split, the tip-end of the top wing dangling down. He'd managed a pretty decent crash. Back at the base in England they'd crow over a salvage landing like that. But he'd still broken her. She might never fly completely straight again, no matter how good the repair.

What an idiot.

"Dad . . . Mr. Newcomb . . . Ma . . . I'm so sorry." He looked over at Patsy, so innocent looking in the coat she'd thrown over her nightgown, her hair cascading loose. All he could end with was a shrug. He hung his head, ashamed, confused. Blood trickled down his nose and splashed onto his hands.

"He's hurt!" Patsy and Lilly rushed to him as Henry's knees buckled. Gently, they brushed back his hair, wiped his face.

"How bad is it?"

"The blood's coming from his forehead."

"He's going to need a stitch or two."

"That's all right, I can do that."

"We've got to get him into the house."

"Can you stand?" Henry felt Patsy slip herself up under

his arm, wrapping it across her slight shoulder. "I'll help you walk."

Clayton stood stock still, glaring.

Lilly took Henry's other arm. She whispered into his ear, "Don't cry, honey lamb. Don't let your dad see you cry." Henry hadn't realized tears were mixing with his blood.

The three stumbled toward the house as Old Man Newcomb started whining, "Ain't you gonna arrest him, sheriff? He destroyed my Jenny."

Inside, the kitchen already smelled of morning coffee and bacon. Lilly had been cooking, preparing for a normal day, while he'd been gallivanting like a crazed fool and nearly killed himself. How could he explain himself to her?

But Lilly didn't ask—just pulled down her first-aid basket to clean and stitch up the gash in his scalp. He bit his tongue to keep from cursing when she dosed it with peroxide. She was quick, though. She'd have made a good doctor, Henry thought fleetingly, if such things were allowed.

When Patsy handed him water and aspirin, he grabbed her hand. No wonder she was afraid of him. He'd disintegrated into a crybaby, a freak. No words came, but his face pleaded forgiveness.

"It's all right," she answered softly.

"The hell it is." Clayton entered, slamming the door so hard all the plates and cups in the china cabinet rattled. He shot his most withering look toward Patsy. "Go home, girl."

Patsy straightened. "No, sir."

Henry almost smiled. But Patsy's refusal infuriated Clayton. "I said, go home. Now!"

"No, sir." Patsy held firm. "Henry's asked me to marry him. So I've a right and a duty to stay here with him."

Clayton's eyes narrowed. "Yeah, I know about that. Another one of his dang-fool ideas. And how'd you answer the boy?"

Patsy hesitated. Henry knew the lag would send Clayton in for the kill. He staggered to his feet. "That's enough, Dad. Patsy had nothing to do with last night."

Clayton stepped close, toe-to-toe with Henry, looking for the fight. Well, maybe this time Henry would give it to him. What did he have to lose?

"Just what was that stunt, boy?" Clayton's voice surprised Henry. There was something beneath the scowl, something new, something akin to concern.

Henry longed to trust that voice, to find the flicker of love he'd seen when he'd stepped out of that taxicab on Thanksgiving Day and his father had realized he was alive. But how could he describe the flashbacks, the mess of past and present, his confusion between waking reality

and nightmare? It was hard enough for Henry to understand how lost he felt while standing right there in his own
home, with the three people he cared about most.

Clayton actually waited.

"Tell us, honey," Lilly coaxed. "What's troubling
you so?"

"Oh, Ma. I just can't forget France. My friends who
died. All those missions where I rained death on people,
on civilians. All the people who helped me and may have
been tortured and killed because of it . . . because of me.
And that little boy, Ma. Pierre. I keep worrying about
where he is. If anyone is helping him."

"But what were you doing in Newcomb's plane?"
Clayton persisted.

"I . . . I . . . I don't know."

Had they been outside, Clayton would have spit on the
ground. "'Don't know' don't cut it, boy."

Henry nodded. For once, Clayton was right. Henry
knew if he told Clayton that he'd gotten drunk on whiskey, he and the sheriff might accept his stealing the plane
as a high-spirited, flyboy prank. But Lilly would be scandal-
ized. And besides, it wasn't true. He'd grown up enough
in the past year to know lying was the coward's way out.

"It's nuts, Dad. But here it is. I think I thought I could
escape it all, find salvation up in the clouds, get myself
right again. The sky always brought me such peace, such

strength. When I fly, I'm free, just like the hawks over the fields. I wish you knew what it's like, Dad. I wish you could see past the farm and the chickens and the weeds and the manure and the banknote."

The last sentence was the mistake.

"Well, I can't see past the banknote, especially with a fool boy who destroys other people's property out joyriding," Clayton snarled. "Here's how I kept you from being arrested. Newcomb says you've ruined that plane. But the army's selling surplus Kaydet trainers for two hundred fifty bucks." He looked over at Lilly. "That old snake sure grabbed the opportunity." He looked back to Henry. "I haven't got two hundred fifty dollars. But you do. How much did that ring cost?"

Lilly gasped. "Oh, no, Clayton, don't make the boy give that up. He . . ."

Henry interrupted her. "Don't get into this, Ma." He knew how often she argued his case with Clayton and how she paid for it in his surliness. And this was justified. He'd screwed up, big-time. He needed to make it right. But Patsy . . . He turned to her.

She held up her hand and smiled, stopping his question. Lord, Henry could live for days on that reassuring smile. "Ask me again later, Henry. Mr. Forester's right." She kissed him on the cheek and left.

Clayton's expression remained grim. "I'll cinch the deal

with Newcomb. He's out there with the sheriff, claiming he'll report Henry to everyone, including the war office, if we don't settle this." He slammed the door again as he left.

Henry eased back into the chair, his head spinning. Lilly knelt beside him. "Henry, honey, I'd give anything to be able to fix things for you. When you were little and hurt or afraid, I could take your hands and say trust me, follow me, I can lead you out of this. But I can't now. You're all grown. My heart's been breaking watching you struggle so, hearing you cry out in your sleep and then getting up to walk off the nightmares."

Henry stared at her. She knew that?

"I can fatten you up, son, but you're the only one who can beat back the demons that have followed you home." She reached over to the table for a newspaper. "I wasn't sure I should show you this. But I see you need to know. I understand your regrets more, honey, reading this. It says that France is worse off now than it was under Hitler's rule in terms of hunger and sickness and lawlessness. It says that Allied bombings destroyed all their railroads and bridges so what food exists can't be shipped. People are starving.

"It's just so awful. And it's going to get worse. When the Soviets liberated a horrible place called Auschwitz, they found thousands . . ." She stopped and shook her head.

"Dear Lord, how is that possible? Hundreds of thousands of people were exterminated. And those who survived are near dead—skeletons, racked with disease. The Allies say there are more camps like it they haven't reached yet. They don't know what to do with the survivors. They have no homes, no families left to return to. Entire villages have been destroyed. Children wander gutted streets not knowing where their parents are."

Lilly's voice grew hoarse and she pushed the paper aside. "Oh, Henry, it is enough to make anyone sick. I understand why you are so worried. Let's pray President Roosevelt and General Eisenhower are wise enough to figure a way out of this horror for those poor people and quick. It's beyond my thinking."

She gently clasped Henry's face so he looked right into her green eyes, the same hue as his. "But I do know this much, honey. Sometimes you get back on your feet better when you're helping someone else stand in the process. The last thing in the world I want is for you to go away again. But I don't think you'll rest easy until you know about that little boy. Maybe . . . maybe you need to go back to France and find Pierre?"

CHAPTER FIVE

Henry walked off the ship's gangplank in clownish high steps, as if his legs expected the earth to lurch up to meet his feet. He dropped his bag and waited for the wharf to stop rocking. Three weeks at sea had left him unused to steady ground. He'd never really acclimated to the ship's decks either. He'd hated the Atlantic crossing, the nights when storm winds and sea waves swirled in titanic convulsions, the boat seeming to pitch and roll in three different directions at once. Give him the sky, give him flat land, forget the ocean.

But he was here—in Marseille, France. His real journey could now begin.

"Problems, son?" His boat's captain walked up steady and straight, easily transitioning from ocean to land. When Henry turned to him with a nauseated face, the old seaman chuckled. "It'll wear off soon. But don't stand here too long. You'll attract trouble. Right now this city is like Chicago in Al Capone's day. When the Allies came through, there was a real bloodletting by the French against people who'd cooperated with the Nazis. Courts are supposed to hear collaboration cases now, but vigilantes still go after people they think cozied up with the Germans. Or seedy types use the rumor that someone was a Nazi-sympathizer to blackmail him. People are pretty desperate for food and clothes. Watch you don't get mugged."

The captain gazed inland to the ragged jigsaws of blown-apart buildings, their hulls left from fires. Here and there a building remained standing. "Look at all that rubble," he muttered.

"Here." He thrust two cartons of Camel cigarettes into Henry's hand. "A bonus. There are twenty packs of cigarettes in these. If you're smart, that'll feed you for a month. Careful who you sell 'em to, though. The cabarets catering to American GIs on leave are your best bet. They're the safest link to the black market." He slapped Henry on the back before walking away.

Clumsily, Henry followed, staggering into the broken city. Marseille shouldn't be this ruined, he thought. The battle for it had only lasted five days. Then the Allies used the port to set up supply lines to the troops as they fought toward Germany. Did all of France look like this?

The April sun was bright and warm, and the Mediterranean Sea behind him a dazzling deep sapphire, so unlike the green-muddy rivers of Tidewater Virginia or the gray foam of the Atlantic. Shading his eyes, Henry looked up at the sandy-stone houses climbing the rocky hills. High on a bleached-out cliff rose a white palace or perhaps a church, an elaborate structure with domes that seemed more like something out of the *Arabian Nights* than Europe. A splash of sunshine reflected off a golden statue on its tallest spire.

Wish Patsy could see this, Henry thought. Even amid this mess, it was prettier than anything she'd ever experienced. Someday, after all this was cleaned up, he'd bring her back to France.

If she'll come with you, a dark voice inside his head jeered.

Henry was awash in such inner arguments these days.
 to come look for Pierre, his mind had been
 of doubts, self-loathing, and anger. This trip
ous. Why couldn't he just screw his head back
 and get on with life? Who in their right mind
 willingly come back to face this manmade hell-on-

 e difficulty of arranging passage alone should have
ped him cold. He'd tried re-upping with the Air Force.
 e corps didn't want him on active duty. He was too thin, too battle-fatigued. Unless, of course, he was willing to

switch theaters, fight some Japs? asked the Richmond air base commander. Henry had explained he wanted to go back to France. Then no, sorry, Henry had already done his part—go home, find a nice girl, and raise a family.

Yeah, right, thought Henry. He bit his tongue from telling the guy how the war had ruined him for that. How his childhood best friend—a girl who'd never been afraid of anything and happily squared off with school bullies and knocked them flat—was spooked by him. That the trip to France was partially sparked by the fact she didn't want to marry him.

Well, at least Patsy was supportive of the journey. At the train station when he left, she'd kissed him and whispered, "Come back to me, Henry."

I'm trying Pats. I'm trying.

It was Patsy who'd heard about a way over for Henry. Charity groups and a new international alliance, called the United Nations, were organizing relief—boatloads of food, clothing, medicines, and livestock. Henry had worked his way over on a merchant boat, funded by a church, carrying hundreds of horses and cows. For a salary of $150, he shoveled manure, fed and watered the animals, and helped birth foals. The sailors made fun of him and the other farm boys on ship. But Henry had felt pretty darn good about being a "seagoing cowboy." These horses and cows were the beginning of new herds, new life—sort of like the cargo of Noah's ark.

Clayton, of course, had thrown a fit, especially since Henry was deserting the farm at planting time. He wouldn't talk to Lilly for days when he learned that she'd suggested Henry go find Pierre. Henry worried over causing Lilly such trouble. "I don't even know what I'm going to do once I'm there, Ma. What is the point of all this anyway?" he asked as they said good-bye. "Pierre and his mother may be just fine. Or they could both be . . . They could all be dead. What am I looking for?"

Lilly answered by buttoning up Henry's coat and brushing his honey-colored hair back, just as she'd always sent him off to school in the morning. "You're looking to help, honey, just as that little boy helped you. It'll be like those quests you were forever telling me about from those King Arthur books you loved. Remember? And in this quest you'll find yourself. Let your heart lead you." She patted his chest. "It's a good heart, sugar."

Well, he'd already done a little bit of good on the boat and felt better for it, especially after reading a newspaper description of the liberation of Paris. Citizens had blockaded neighborhood streets and thrown homemade grenades at Germans trying to hold the city. By that point, Parisians were so hungry that when an old thin horse the Resistants were using to cart supplies fell down dead of exhaustion, housewives carrying kitchen knives rushed out of their apartments into the battle's crossfire to carve the carcass up into steaks.

France needed new horses. Given the state of Marseille, France obviously needed a lot of things.

Henry was putting himself into a bad situation, though. He'd have to be careful. He really didn't have papers to be in France. The livestock ship had docked in Trieste, Italy. It was going straight back to Baltimore for another load and the crew wasn't allowed shore leave. Henry had jumped ship and lucked into finding work on a boat making the sail into Marseille. He'd have to avoid MPs, the military police, patrolling cities in which Americans maintained bases or were granted leave. Several U.S. transports, supply ships, and a Red Cross boat were anchored in the harbor behind him. He'd need to get out of Marseille quickly and head northeast toward the Vercors, the mountainous plateau leading to the Alps and Switzerland, where he'd left Pierre.

A gang of boisterous American soldiers in uniform khaki rounded the corner. Henry hurried onto a narrow, cobblestone street, picking his way over heaps of debris from blasted buildings, startled to hear the sound of laughter and a flute from inside one of the scarred houses. He threaded his way toward the city's center, stepping in and out of blazing sunlight and dank shadows cast down alley-thin streets.

The stench of sewage mixed with the smell of garlic and fish. Sewer lines must have been blown, too. Henry held his sleeve to his nose as he walked.

After a while he came to a square, miraculously unscathed, dotted with thin iron chairs and white-clothed tables the French always put outside their cafés. Radio music drifted out from the restaurants. Almond trees bloomed. Their delicate pink blossoms obliterated the stink of the streets he'd crossed. Suddenly Henry was hungry, starving in a way he hadn't felt since boarding the rocking boats. The dozen tins of Spam his mother had stuffed in his bag wouldn't satisfy this hunger. Henry headed to a bistro, crowded with men in baggy corduroys and what looked like GI jackets stripped of their insignia.

As he approached, one of the men jumped up to grab a waiter by the collar. *"Quatre-vingts francs pour cette soupe dégoûtante?"* he shouted about the cost and the quality of the soup. *"Je ne paie pas!"* He shook the waiter.

Henry stopped. He understood the actions to be like a school punk shaking down a weaker kid for lunch money. The irate customer shoved the waiter and pulled a revolver from his belt.

People at surrounding tables jumped up, knocking over their chairs to back away. But once out of the gun's immediate range, they stood, waiting, probably not wanting to abandon their food, clearly used to such confrontations.

Henry froze and began to tremble.

"Tu donnes aux boches tes meilleurs saucissons et tes meilleurs gâteaux!"

The waiter cowered and shook his head, saying, no, he never waited on the Nazis. He didn't give them cakes and sausages. *"Pas moi, monsieur."*

Hearing the shouts, the owner appeared. He was short, stout, bald, and surprisingly bold, waving them off. *"Arrêtez! Criminels!"*

The gunman's friends turned on him. Laughing, they called him a *collabo*, a filthy collaborator. They took turns shoving him. They knew he had cash inside, Nazi money, *le prix du sang*, blood money.

One of them pushed a gun against the owner's temple.

But the owner faced down his robber. He wasn't about to empty his cash register for him.

The gunman cocked his pistol. *"Ça me va,"* he shrugged. *"Au revoir, collabo."*

"Non, non, non!" A woman rushed out and shoved a fistful of bills into the gunman's hand. He grinned. Slowly, he released the owner, picked up his bowl, and drank its soup down. Wiping his mouth with his sleeve, he swaggered off with his companions.

The rest of the café's patrons resumed their seats. They ate. They talked. Like the scene was nothing more than a brief cloudburst that had passed.

★ ★ ★

But Henry remained glued to his spot, sweating, feeling a Lugar pistol pressed against his own forehead, the cold *O* of its barrel boring into his flesh. *Once a thing is no longer of use to me, I rid myself of it.* The Gestapo officer's face—fair, sleek, sharp—appeared, huge, an inch from Henry's. The thin lips twisted with contempt. Henry felt hot breath in his ear. *Your courage is impressive, but ultimately pointless. I will break you.*

Henry closed his eyes and prepared for the blast. *Go ahead, you SOB. Shoot. I won't tell you anything about Madame Gaulloise or Pierre. I won't.*

KA-BANG!

Henry clutched his head to hold together the blown-open pieces of his skull. But the Nazi had shot wide. *Ha! Shooting you would have ended our games prematurely, American. You will not get off that easily.*

Henry could smell the acrid explosion, could hear the sneering laughter, could feel Nazi hands grab him and drag him to an interrogation room.

No, no, not there. NO!

Henry surfaced back to Marseille. He flopped into a chair and was rubbing his hands together to stop their shaking. He caught his breath, horrified. A small girl was standing right in front of him, holding a tulip. She was trying to hand him the flower. Was she real? Henry looked around. All the café diners were staring at him. Conversation had ceased. Had they witnessed his crazy hallucination? *Get a grip, boy. Quick.* If Henry wasn't careful, these people might throw him into a French loony bin. Maybe that's where he belonged.

"Toutes mes condoléances pour votre perte. C'est surement un moment très difficile." The child spoke in a sweet, sad voice. She was very sorry for his loss? Could she see into his soul, see how lost he was?

Like coming out of a fog, Henry began to hear things around him. The radio's music had broken into a broadcast—something about FDR. Henry was still too unnerved to follow what was being said.

The child repeated herself.

Henry shook his head. "I don't understand."

The owner approached. "President Roosevelt has died," he said in accented and formal English. "We mourn with you. It is a great loss for the world."

CHAPTER SIX

The owner invited Henry back to the small kitchen and brought him a bowl of soup. It was half-full, the broth thin, but it was chock-full of fish. The spicy aroma was wonderful. "Had I more butter, tomatoes, salt, the bouillabaisse would be better," the owner apologized. "But this is my best. I save this for *mes amis*. Much better than the crow soup I fed that vermin." He grinned. "Each day that gangster goes to a café to eat free by threats. He deals in stolen American petrol and uniforms. A very bad man. So I give the blackbird dinner to him. Filthy RMA."

His wife cut Henry a thick slice of coarse, brown bread and sat down next to him. He nodded his thanks to her. "What's an 'RMA,' *monsieur*?"

The owner's voice filled with disdain. "An RMA is a 'resistant of the month of August.' The RMAs collabo-

42

rated with the Vichy, the puppet government Hitler set in France. Then, when the Allies approached and Paris rose up in rebellion, they suddenly changed their allegiance. They put on the Free French armband and followed General de Gaulle. How you say, 'turncoat'?"

Henry hesitated, spoon midair. The man had been so sad over FDR's death that Henry had followed him to the kitchen without thinking. But hadn't the gunman accused this man of being a collaborator? Henry lowered his spoon back into the bowl and looked down at the table. His appetite was suddenly gone. What if his host had turned over Resistants, the *maquis*, to the Gestapo, like whoever betrayed Pierre's mother?

The woman frowned and glanced up at her husband. *"Il n'aime pas la bouillabaisse."*

She looked so disappointed that Henry's manners got the best of him. *"Non, madame. C'est superb."*

"Ahhhhh. *Vous parlez français?"*

"Un peu, monsieur, un petit peu." A very little.

The owner leaned up against the white stucco wall and folded his arms across his chest. His expression clouded. "So you understood what that filth said of me. Little is black and white, *monsieur*. The world is full of grays, in-betweens. Especially France right now. Yes, I fed the Nazis, *les boches*. I swallowed my hate and served the swine. That was so I heard things to pass on to the Resistance *maquis*. So I had money to feed the Allied airmen I hid in my cellar—British, American, Canadian, Russian. All of them safe to the Pyrenees because of the ruse my wife and I kept.

"But after Marseille was won, we were arrested as *collabos*. I would have been shot except one of my comrades, a known *maquisard*, was in the next room, interrogating others. I recognized his voice through the wall. I shouted for him. He told them what I had done, what we had risked. We ran to where they held my wife. They were about to tar her beautiful face with a swastika."

The owner's own face reddened. "They have made many such mistakes in their hurry for revenge. For some of us, the best cover for our Resistance work was to be friendly to the Germans."

It was this statement that made Henry believe the restaurateur. Madame Gaulloise had gathered money to buy Henry's escape by gambling at a casino in the company of a Nazi official. The fat German had been completely infatuated with her, and she had used that. Henry could hear her silken voice: *I play a high-society coquette to disarm my enemy and to keep myself a mystery. They think they know me for something I am not.*

Henry fought off the sickening image of the pork-sized Aryan interrogating the sophisticated woman who had arranged his trek to freedom.

"My ship captain told me that collaborators are tried in

court now," said Henry. "Why don't the police stop men like those guys who hassled you from falsely accusing people?"

The owner snorted. "The purge is run by people desperate to prove their allegiance to Free France. The RMAs denounce fellow collaborators with the same joy they once turned over the *maquis* to the Gestapo. They go after easy targets—maids, cooks, servants, laundresses who worked for the Nazi occupiers to feed their children. These hungry workers were cowards, yes. But traitors? No. They did not help the Reich deport Jews or capture political prisoners. The simple people who cannot afford lawyers go to jail while businessmen who dined with Nazis and made millions of francs building things for them are left alone. Vichy officials—who enforced Hitler's anti-Jew laws—are still judges, mayors. De Gaulle pardons many to keep the framework of government intact."

The owner was growing agitated. "This is not what I fought for! We must overturn everything and start a new republic free of Hitler's puppets, free of corruption, free of class prejudice and hate for Jews. . . ."

His wife had inched toward him, understanding not the meaning but the tone of his English words. Gently she took his hand. He stopped. *"Pardon, monsieur.* One hardship follows another." He rubbed his face clear of anger and sat down at the table, drawing his wife to a chair as well.

"Eat"—he motioned to Henry—"and tell me of Harry

Truman. Roosevelt's courage led the world. Can this man do the same?"

"To be completely honest, I don't know much about him," Henry admitted. "I think Mr. Truman was a senator from Missouri before becoming vice president. But don't worry. The war will be over soon, *monsieur*. Our boys are closing in on Berlin now. The Nazis can't hold out much longer. Back home they're saying the war in Europe will be over in a month. That'll just leave the Japanese."

"Yes, perhaps, *Dieu soit loué*," the owner crossed himself. Then he frowned, puzzled. Clearly the question just came to him. "Why are you here?"

Hearing his host's sincerity, his rage and disappointment, Henry realized that in France people would understand his pain and confusion better than anyone could back home, where the worst day-to-day complaints had been about rationing or having to use blackout curtains to hide city lights from German U-boats cruising the East Coast. Henry let his story tumble out: of being shot down and saved by the ancient teacher, of coming in and out of Switzerland, of the elegant Madame Gaulloise connecting him to the ratline escape route, of Pierre and his mother's arrest, of Henry's betrayal at the Spanish border, of the Gestapo, Claudette, the old German sergeant who ultimately released him, and his surprise homecoming.

Henry leaned toward the man. "The *maquis* in the

Morvan told me the Nazis hit the Vercors hard after I left Pierre. Bombed it because of their resistance. I just want to make sure the boy is all right." Henry pulled up short, realizing how naïve he sounded. As if he could walk up to Pierre's house, knock on the door, and find him there, safe and sound. Look at Marseille, its devastation. Embarrassed, Henry sat back in his chair.

For a long moment, the Frenchman gazed at Henry. "You are not like the other Americans now in Marseille. The ones we see drink too much, shout too much, and whistle at our innocents, as if they were all cabaret girls. You will stay here tonight. Tomorrow I will put you on a train to Lyon. It will stop in Valence. You climb the mountains from there." He paused, muttering to himself more than to Henry. *"Il me faut quelque chose pour soudoyer le chef de train."*

A bribe for the conductor?

Henry reached into his bag and pulled out one of the two Camel cigarette cartons the ship captain had given him. "Will this do?"

"Oui," the Frenchman laughed, clapping his hands. But then he sobered and added, "It is a good thing that God sent you to me, *monsieur*. If you had pulled that out to show most people in Marseille, you would be lying on the ground now, a large bump on your head."

CHAPTER SEVEN

Henry flattened himself against a windowpane, trying to create space between himself and the other men crammed into the passageway of the train car. He knew he smelled horrible. His blond hair was dark with grease. He hadn't properly washed since sailing out of Baltimore. The restaurateur had apologized, but coal was in such short supply, he had just enough to heat hot water for baths every third day. That morning was not the day.

He also couldn't prepare much of a breakfast for Henry. "One egg can cost thirty francs," he said with a sigh. "I could not cook them for you if I had them. Electricity is rationed *aussi*. It is turned on for only one hour mid-day so we may cook dinner." Instead he had given Henry a hunk of bread and cold coffee—the worst tasting coffee Henry had ever tasted. Thinking of the crow soup,

Henry didn't ask of what the coffee was made.

He kicked himself for not sticking a can of instant coffee into his bag before leaving home. He could have made a small fortune off that, he bet. The thought shamed him. But the price of eggs panicked Henry. GIs were getting 50 francs to the dollar, a great exchange rate for Americans. But that still meant the price of an egg could be a whopping 60¢. Back home the Richmond grocer who sold their eggs charged customers 58¢ for a dozen. Henry only had $196 with him—$150 from taking care of the livestock, $5 from working the short sail from Trieste to Marseille, and $41 from the tin can of "mad money" that Lilly painstakingly saved a penny, a nickel at a time. How long would that last him if he had to pay for a single egg what a dozen should cost?

Henry's stomach rumbled loudly. So did that of the man squashed next to him.

Henry was in a pickle, for sure. It wasn't like he could just find work here in France. All its people were desperately trying to make do, laboring for *centimes*. The café owner's little girl had left at dawn to work as a *queutière*, a placeholder. There was a rumor that a poultry shipment was due into town sometime in the next few days. Women were already queuing at butcher shops, counting out their ration points. The café owner's daughter would stand in line all day for someone else to earn a penny.

Thank goodness Henry hadn't had to pay for his train ticket. The café owner had whispered into the conductor's ear and pressed three packs of Camels into his hand and Henry was waved into line. Henry wouldn't have to buy a ticket, he explained, out of respect for the late President Roosevelt. Henry wondered how far the French deference for FDR and lust for American tobacco would get him.

Henry was glad to have the windowpane to lean against. Many of the train's travelers were forced to stand, swaying with its rocking, keeping upright mainly because of the press of so many bodies. The train from Marseille to Lyon to Paris was one of the few running. Half the rail lines still weren't open, bombed by the Allies or cut by the *maquis* the previous June to make it impossible for Hitler to reinforce his troops fighting on the Normandy beaches after D-day with fresh soldiers from Germany. The Resistance had blown up thousands of locomotives and train cars and torn apart miles of tracks.

Inside the sitting compartment, wooden benches that typically held three or four were crammed with six. But the French were so thin, they easily packed themselves like sardines. Sadly, Henry noted how quiet they were. There was a grayness to their faces. Their clothes showed signs of multiple mendings. They didn't look like a liberated people. But that would come, wouldn't it? Once Hitler surrendered?

The trip dragged as the train limped along slowly on diesel instead of coal-fueled steam. It chugged away from Marseille, passing marshes and white beaches to the west. The sight of them triggered memories of the truck ride he and Billy had taken toward the Pyrenees—the vast mountains bordering Spain they had to cross to freedom—where everything had gone wrong.

Now there was something he had meant to do—write Billy's mother and sisters in Philadelphia and tell them how brave Billy had been in the end. He needn't let on what a pain in the neck Billy'd been before that. How much he'd whined about food when the *maquis* fed them what little they had. Well, there'd be time for that, Henry reassured himself. Nothing would change the fact that poor Billy was dead. His family could use a few good words about him whenever, maybe even more so after the war ended and American boys who had survived came home in droves.

Henry's hands began to shake. Would Billy's family believe him when he told them how hard he'd tried to bring Billy home? Should he have done more? Instantly, he was on the storm-wracked mountaintop, struggling to drag a bleeding Billy away from the German patrol.

"Hurry, Billy, they're coming!"

"Heir entlang!" Rat-tat-tat-tat.

"I'm hit, Hank. Oh, God. Hank, help me!"

"I'll pull you, Billy. Hang on to me."

"Heir entlang!"

"Let go of me, Hank. Leave me. I'm dying."

"No. We're both going home, Billy. I can carry you. Put your arm around my neck."

"Hank, go on. You can't help me now. Get home to that pretty girl of yours."

Remembering the sight of Billy's brown eyes going glassy, Henry covered his face and whispered, "She doesn't want me, Billy. Maybe you should have lived instead of me."

"Pardon, monsieur?"

Henry snapped back to the train. He cleared his throat, coughed, and waved his hand as if he had simply choked on something. He tried to make himself as small and inconspicuous as possible and focused on the French dialogue around him to keep his mind clear of memories.

His understanding of the language was improved a bit from having spent so many months last year with the *maquis*. But it was still pretty bare-boned. As before, Henry caught a few words here, a phrase there. It was like working a cryptogram or trying to find the hidden meaning in an acrostic poem. At least this time, he wasn't having to assess whether the person in front of him was going to save him or sell him. What a nightmare it had been last year to catch the words *Allemand* for German, *soldat* for soldier, *frontière* for border, and *argent* for money and wonder whether the speaker planned to gather money to bribe German soldiers to get Henry across the border safely, or to lure Henry to the border and turn him over for a good price to the Nazis waiting there. That was precisely what happened to him in the Pyrenees, and what had happened to Billy.

Henry shuddered. This trip was already bringing back all sorts of things he had managed to bury. If anything, the flashbacks were becoming more frequent. Maybe exposing himself to all this wasn't such a great idea after all.

One of the train travelers clutched a long baguette. His friend asked how much the bread had cost. The answer made the questioner curse and speculate that pretty soon he'd have to sell his house to feed his family.

"Au moins t'as toujours ta maison, mon ami."

The man nodded. *"Oui, c'est vrai."* At least his house, unlike his friend's, was still standing.

"Les américains donnent des oranges aux prisonniers allemands."

"Des oranges!" Grimly, the man joked that for one of

the oranges the American army was feeding the German POWs he would give up not only his house but also his entire village. His son's muscles ached, and he was weak, his teeth were loose. He worried about scurvy. His son needed oranges to prevent the disease—more than a Nazi murderer.

It took a moment for Henry to piece together what the men were saying. When he translated why they resented American troops feeding German POWs well, Henry felt his face burn with embarrassment. He turned to the window to avoid being recognized as an American. What a tragedy, he thought, that the United States treating POWs decently would make the French bitter. But far worse was the fact French children were suffering so from lack of food. Hunger was clearly the next enemy facing U.S. troops.

Henry kept his gaze out the window as the train ran along the wide, wild currents of the Rhône. It passed a dozen bridges blown on their eastern edge, beams and cable still dangling into the water, bricks strewn hundreds of yards from the blast of plastique explosives. The *maquis* had been very thorough in their work. Or perhaps it was the handiwork of retreating Germans.

The landscape reflected Henry's state of mind—all the basics were there, but the things that made everyday life and getting back to normal possible were broken, disconnected. He wondered how the French would rebuild. Could they repair what remained, or would they have to tear it all down and begin anew? Which was better—reconstruction that openly contained scars from the past, or brand-new architecture that wiped clean a painful history? Which was stronger, more quickly accomplished? If the second method were chosen, what hole would be deep enough to bury all that rubble? Or all that pain?

In early afternoon, the train chugged into Montélimar. One more stop to Valence. The train jostled with people getting on and off. Their shoes—still soled with wood instead of rubber, which had been requisitioned for tires during the Occupation—clacked loudly on the iron-grate stairs.

A pretty young woman stepped into Henry's train car. He noticed her at first because she didn't seem half-starved like everyone else. She had a healthy voluptuousness that made him blush a bit. Her face was round, her nose long and straight, her eyes large and almond-shaped. She had that idiosyncratic French beauty about her that Henry had first come to appreciate in Claudette, the young, fiery Resistant who took him in after he escaped the Gestapo. He winced, remembering how he met Claudette—stealing fruit from her orchard, starving, broken. Her yellow-green, catlike eyes had looked at him with such disdain.

As the girl neared, Henry noticed bruising around her

cheekbones. She nervously tugged on the colorful silk scarf she'd tied round her head.

"*La femme au turban*," a man beside Henry hissed.

Henry glanced at him in surprise. The man had been silent, his eyes half closed the whole trip. It was like a giant snake had awakened. He nudged the man next to him, repeating the phrase "turban woman" and adding *collabo horizontale*.

That man passed the nudge and the words: *la femme au turban*. Instantly all the men were on alert, sneering.

The young woman looked at each one, defiantly at first. She turned red and then very, very pale. She backed her way out of the compartment and spent the next hour clinging to the hand bar of the platform linking the cars, her skirt whipping around her in the wind. At one point her scarf was blown loose. She caught it before it flew away. She was bald.

Now Henry understood. She'd been shaven. Her scarf, her "turban," was like the scarlet letter in that Hawthorne novel he'd read in high school. It was the clear marker that the girl had had a romance with a German soldier. Until her hair grew back, she'd be shunned—or worse.

Claudette had threatened to stab a teenager accused of such dalliances. Claudette's passions—loyalty, love, and hatred alike—ran hot. That trait both attracted and repulsed Henry. In many ways, Claudette reminded him of Patsy—a Patsy who was boiled down, distilled. If Patsy had been faced with the same kind of dangers and tragedies Claudette endured, she might have condensed into the same fury.

Henry's thoughts went to a recent conversation with Patsy—a painful one. "Sometimes when you kiss me it feels like you're searching for something, Henry," she'd whispered, uncharacteristically unsure of herself. "Almost like your mind is elsewhere, on something—on someone—else. Henry, " her voice grew hoarse as she asked, "was there someone else in France?"

No, Pats. That kiss with Claudette, that night by the Morvan pond—that was searching for you.

He should have told her that, but he'd just fibbed instead, saying no, there wasn't. Truth be known, he did think often of Claudette. He'd stopped her from attacking the accused girl and sacrificed himself to save Claudette from being captured, and these were the only actions he was proud of during his run for freedom. Had Claudette knifed the girl, Claudette would have become as pitiless as the Gestapo—she'd be ruined. Henry thought back to the old German sergeant who had let him go. That kind of mercy, that kind of respect for life, was needed now to restore peace, to rebuild.

But maybe that was easier said than done here, where people had been tormented daily, starved, and set upon one another by the Nazis like in a cockfight—neighbors denouncing one another for revenge, for bread, to save their own skin, to be rid of people they thought troublesome or annoying or racially inferior. Given the suspicions, the residual and justified anger still smoldering in France, it would take real courage to stand up to a mob bent on revenge. Henry could see that their hatred would easily turn on anyone disagreeing or arguing against them.

At Valence, the turbaned girl jumped to the ground before the train pulled to a complete stop. She hurried through the station. Henry was glad to see her slip away safely. No one noticed her because there was a huge commotion along the tracks. People had surrounded a horse-drawn grocery wagon. They were waving sticks, brooms, umbrellas, and shouting.

"*Du beurre!*" a man from the crowd called into the train. The cart had butter in it. The food ministry had ordered it shipped to Paris, to be sold there. The mob was trying to stop it. "*C'est notre beurre! Venez! Aidez-nous!*"

The man's cries sparked a small riot. Henry was knocked about by passengers shouting and pushing to the exit. They rushed to the butter cart, shrieking at the driver to sell the butter to them, rather than loading it onto the train for Paris.

"*Moi!*" They shoved and elbowed one another to be first.

"Moi d'abord!" There was a madness among the people, a desperation that sickened Henry.

For butter.

He waded through the crowd and hurried to the edge of the train station to get his bearings. Far in the distance, on the eastern horizon, rose a long jagged shadow, the purple-gray outline of the Vercors's mountains and the pre-Alps behind them. Henry caught his breath with relief. Toward the hills, there would be space. Toward the hills, he would be free of the smells, the panic bred by hungry people crammed too close together, squabbling over the same scrap of food.

Henry had faith in the countryside, faith in good land providing hope and sustenance, faith that a people fed would be more merciful to one another, faith that in the hills that kissed the clouds, he would find Pierre.

Henry shouldered his bag and walked away from the chaos the war had left in its wake.

Chapter Eight

"Marchez!"

Henry remembered the first night—a year and a treacherous journey ago—that the *maquis* set him along its ratline. No instructions other than turn left at a fork. *Walk.* Someone would pick him up. Who? Where? How will I know him?

Walk. That was all the gruff *maquis* fighter would answer.

Henry had walked through the night, his only companions moonlight and fear. He'd threaded his way along a two-foot-slim path of stones scratched into the white cliffs, so high they felt more part of the sky than of the earth. One false step and he'd have plummeted hundreds of feet, the only thing to catch him a forest of firs a parachute drop below.

Walk.

He'd made it down the crags into a valley of meadows, and crept through a slumbering village, barely breathing for fear of waking a dog that would howl an alarm. He had jumped back in terror from a poster of a German soldier, his nerves so raw he mistook the image for a person. Continuing, he made it out the other end and along the road some more. Finally, finally, as dawn broke and his confidence broke, a small figure had walked up the road, taken his hand, and led him to a safe house. Pierre—all of eight years old but with the courage of a medal-valor soldier.

Walk.

This would be easy. It was daylight for one thing, and the twenty miles it must be to the base of the mountain range were flat and beautiful. Stretching out around him were miles of chest-high sunflowers. Their faces were just beginning to stretch skyward and to open, bursts of gold, as if the sun had sprinkled bits of itself to the earth. He felt the distress of Marseille, the train ride, and the food riot slide off him.

No sweat. I'll walk. My pleasure.

Henry set a steady pace. Back home he'd made the two miles to school in forty minutes, so he should make the mountains in about seven hours. He tried not to rush with impatience, knowing that would tire and ultimately slow him. He'd have to camp out that night. But by tomorrow he'd be in Vassieux, Pierre's village. Tomorrow, he'd know.

Henry let the land seduce him, glancing around, not warily as in the previous year—searching shadows, trees, rocks for Nazis—but with a tourist's sense of awe. Virginia was gorgeous when it greened up in spring, but the colors here were so much more vibrant. The gold-green carpet of sunflowers reminded Henry of one of the paintings Madame Gaulloise had hanging in her aristocratic home. It'd been a landscape of illusion: from afar, a wash of colors, like dappled sunlight on water, revealing ponds, flowers, trees, clouds. Up close the picture spread itself into a blur of thick dots and smears of paint. Impressionism, she'd called the style of painting.

Madame. Henry couldn't let his mind wander there. There was another incredibly brave person he had endangered. He didn't see how her quick-witted playacting could possibly have saved her from the Gestapo once they had her. The only solace there was that she had made the decision to be a freedom-fighter for herself, as an adult. Could an eight-year-old boy really understand what he risked, what he was facing if caught?

Henry shook his head to shake out the thoughts. He didn't want to mourn right now. He wanted to hope, hope that just on the other side of the mountain he would find

Pierre, safe, and therefore find himself. Then he could go home, whole, home to Patsy, ready. Henry forced himself to whistle a happy tune—his carefree loudness another luxury of liberation.

Three hours of warm sun and watching small birds flitting among the flowers to hunt bugs brought Henry to Chabeuil. He decided to skirt the town's edges. Not much longer to go now. The mountains were rearing huge ahead, three thousand feet of ragged rock, like the sawtooth walls of a castle-fort, guarding the entrance to heaven.

From inside the town, he heard playful shouts of children and a ball bouncing against a wall. He smelled wood fires and meat being smoked. He saw small, square gardens, neatly lined with sprouts of lettuce and bean plants. Life was beginning anew here. He felt like skipping.

But on the mountain end of the town, Henry pulled up short. Ahead of him were balls of tangled barbed wire, the fence posts long gone for firewood. Huge, thick ruts furrowed the ground, stretching for miles toward the Vercors. Henry knew what had cut so deeply into the earth—tanks. But what horrified him was the sight of a long strip of paving and the scattershot debris of planes along its edges. The hulls had been burned, the engines ripped open for parts, the gun racks stripped, but Henry could still recognize the outline. Nazi Junkers.

He looked up at the mountains, thinking air speed. *Sweet Jesus.* It would have taken only five minutes for those Luftwaffe planes to cross over into . . .

Henry started to run—run along the flight path he knew could deliver a fiery death to Pierre's people within minutes of takeoff.

Of course, he couldn't run far. The road soon turned into a hard upward slope. His legs slowed to a walk, an aching scramble, as he leaned forward for balance. With dread he noticed a deserted Mercedes-Benz, pockmarked with bullet holes; an overturned truck, gutted; emptied strings of machine gun cartridges; a little further, crushed cans of gasoline and long, ragged scorch marks scarring the land. *Idiot! What did you expect?*

Henry climbed up into winds and looked back to a world laid out in a serene patchwork of lavenders, golds, and greens. The sun was setting low, beneath him. Where he stood clouds were gathering around him, wet, cold. He felt none of the joy he usually would when wisps of cumulus brushed his hands. He was in for it in terms of weather. By the time he made it to the crest, it was raining, water streaming down the road. He recognized the pass, Col de la Bataille, and found its tunnel through the rock. Huddled inside, he watched lightning crackle along the plain. He couldn't yet see into the mountain valley on the other side, the green pocket where Pierre's farm lay. His view was blocked by a thick forest—the woods where he and Pierre had met up with the local *maquis*, hurrying to retrieve guns and chocolates parachuted in by the British.

Henry's worries thundered in his head. Would the priest, the monks, have been able to shelter Pierre during a Nazi air raid? Surely the Nazis wouldn't have gone after everyone, not women, not children. Chabeuil looked intact. He paused in his thinking, remembering the brutal raid on Pierre's home and how the Milice had gunned down the ancient grandfather without asking him a single question.

Henry made himself watch the storm. After months of agonized speculation, he'd gotten within a few hours of discovering the truth of Pierre's circumstances. Henry had at least learned one thing while on the run—to hunker down and wait things out when he had no other options.

He sat down with the rock at his back, glancing back and forth between the two tunnel entrances, instinctively checking his camp perimeters, as they'd been taught in basic training. Such habits were dying hard. Henry pulled out a can of Spam, twisted the key along its top to roll back the tin, and forced himself to swallow.

CHAPTER NINE

Seven white crosses.

They were the first things Henry saw as he came out of the cool, sweet-smelling beech-wood shadows of Forêt de Lente. The bright sunrise cast a crimson glow on the roadside graves. He rounded the bend in the gravel path. Five more wooden crosses—the dead obviously laid to rest where they had fallen. There, another ten. And just beyond, a farmhouse charred, nothing but a rectangle of sooty stone.

Henry filled with dread.

After ten more minutes of scrambling down slopes, Henry came to the rim of the Vassieux valley. Beneath him should have been a lush green cup of fields and farms, wildflowers and sleepy cattle, ruled in the center by a little village of creamy houses with cheery pink-tiled roofs that were nestled around a church—its bell ringing out the hour, clear and sweet, rejoicing in another day.

Instead there was silence. A wide field of white crosses. A thin dirt runway, pockmarked with bomb craters. Skeletons of small aircraft that looked like German gliders.

And where the village should have been—alive with roosters crowing, children yawning over cups of frothy warm milk, mothers humming as they poached eggs—was rubble.

Oh, no. No, no, no. Henry shaded his eyes against the horizontal sunlight, and scanned up the valley to where he knew Pierre's cluster of farm buildings should be. *Please. Let it be there.*

Gone. Everything gone. As if God, large as the mountains, had stood on that ridge and rolled boulders down into the valley, smashing and crushing things the way a bowling ball would glass. And yet the revolting truth was that it had been men, methodically moving from house to house, bent on the destruction of other human beings. Henry could imagine the cries, the pleas, the refusals, the machine-gun fire, flames catching hold of timber, houses collapsing.

He crouched, hugging his knees to fight off vomiting. What should he do now? Who was left to help him find Pierre? Was Pierre alive to be found?

From the distance came the faint sound of gears shifting and grinding, an engine backfiring from a charcoal converter. Henry lifted his head. A small silver square of car was threading its way into the broken remains of Vassieux from the opposite side of the valley.

Henry stood. Perhaps the driver would know something that could help him. He descended into the ruins.

Henry found the car parked alongside the field of crosses. A man had gotten out to stand among the graves. He was short, square, and solid like a bulldog, with gray hair and a thick black moustache. He held his brimmed beret in one hand, a crooked walking stick in the other. His hefty mountain boots, woolen pants, sweater-vest, and flannel shirt rolled up bare, muscular arms showed him to be a Vercors man. Henry felt a twinge of hope. This man had survived the German attack. That meant others must have, too. He trotted up shouting, not noticing that the man's face was awash in tears.

So startled, the man's sorrow switched instantly to suspicion. *"Qui êtes-vous?"* he snapped. *"Qu'est-ce que vous voulez?"*

Henry faltered at the man's belligerence. In stammering French, he explained he was looking for a boy.

The man's frown turned murderous. "You are American?" he growled.

"Yes, *monsieur.*" Henry was thrilled—the man spoke English. Hopefully he would have the same reverence for

FDR and be as helpful as the café owner. "I'm trying to find a boy, a boy who lived on a farm"—he turned away to point up the road—"about a mile up, near . . ."

Henry didn't see the hit coming. The first blow knocked him to the ground. The second strike of the walking stick split open the gash Lilly had sewn shut. The third exploded pain in his ribs. The fourth, he caught.

Holding fast to the stick, Henry yanked the man down and jumped to his feet. But the Frenchman lunged at Henry's knees, tackling him back to the dirt. Choking on dust, Henry wrestled the writhing man, trying to push him off. The man was strong. He kicked, punched, all the while snarling, "Why you not come? Why you not come?"

Taking everything he had to roll the man over and off, Henry shoved and back-crawled. He staggered to his feet and held up his fists, just the way Clayton had taught him to box. "Come on. Now I'm ready for you."

But he wasn't. The man was far faster than Henry anticipated. With a rush and a shoulder to Henry's gut, the Frenchman knocked him to his knees again. Henry cried out in pain, feeling a horrible catch in his breath.

"Arrêtez! Arrêtez, patron! Nous avons eu assez de carnage!"

His head spinning, vision blurred, Henry collapsed. Lying on the ground, he could make out another pair of feet running toward him, kicking up chalky ash. Soft hands sat him up and, for a moment, Henry could focus on the babyish, pale face and the concerned voice of a second man who knelt beside him. *"Pouvez-vous vous lever?"*

Could Henry stand? He tried and failed.

Instead he felt himself pulled to his feet and walked to the shade of a burned-out house and lowered to lean against the wall. There was something familiar about this second man's face. Something. But all Henry could focus on was the incomprehensible argument going on above him between the baby-faced man and Henry's attacker.

"C'est un d'eux! Ils ont permis le massacre de nos gens!"

"Cet homme n'est pas responsable de ça, patron."

"Quelqu'un doit payer!"

Bloodied, shaken, confused, Henry could only understand the words *massacre* and someone having to pay for it. The memory of the Gestapo beating him unconscious gripped his mind and twisted the moment into a mess of past, present, and fearful imagination.

"Hit him. Schlag ihn! *Again!* Schlag ihn nochmal! Hard! . . . *You cannot win this game, American.* Schlag ihn hart! . . . *See that over there? We call that the bathtub. Your head goes in the water—over and over and over again—however long it takes for me to get the information I want. But first . . . hit him again—hard.* Nochmal! Härter!"

No, it's not real. Henry fought against the daytime nightmare. He focused on the words flying around him. *French words. French.* "It's not the Gestapo. It's not the Gestapo.

It's not the Gestapo," he muttered louder and louder, chanting to stop his slide into the insanity of memory and paranoia.

The French conversation stopped.

"*Mon Dieu.*" The Vercors man's face came into view. "What have I done?" Henry felt hands gently passing over his rib cage. "I may break a rib. I drive you to doctor. *Aidez-moi à le soulever.*"

Henry felt himself carried and laid in the back of the car. Wind rushed over his face as the car took off. Each bounce and jolt along the rough road felt like another blow to his ribs. Henry kept his eyes on the sky, lifting his spirit to the clouds just as he had the day he was taken out to be shot.

"It's not the Gestapo. It's not the Gestapo. It's not the Gestapo."

CHAPTER TEN

"You must forgive *le patron*. Since July, his grief haunts him."

Henry sat in a tiny, incense-scented church, one of the few buildings standing in the nearby town of Saint Martin. A doctor was circling bandages tightly around his chest, setting his ribs in case one had cracked. The Vercors man and the pale-faced one were sitting outside the door, under a tree charred along one side and blooming on the other.

The doctor continued, "He says that when he heard you call out against the Gestapo, he realized his madness."

Henry shifted uncomfortably, ashamed of his outburst. How crazy was he going to get? "About that, doctor, I can explain. . . ." Henry trailed off. How could he explain?

"No need. Those of us who survived Nazi brutality are all a little mad. *Le patron* was a sergeant in the Great War, a union leader, like a father. That is why we called him *le patron*, boss. As leader of our *maquis*, he feels responsible for all the deaths, the burning. That is why his rage overcomes him sometimes. *Vous comprenez?*"

Henry nodded. He certainly understood sorrows causing wild actions. "But why is he so angry at Americans?"

"Because he agreed to 'Operation *Montagnards*.' He knew how the plan endangered us. How terrible Nazi reprisals would be if it failed. But he trusted General de Gaulle and the Allies."

"Operation *Montagnards?*" All battle plans seemed to have had code titles. "Does *montagnard* mean mountain?"

The doctor sighed with a weariness so deep Henry knew he'd never forget the sound of it. "Yes. The plan was that when the Allies attacked the Normandy beaches on D-day, our *maquis* would establish a mountain fortress here, cut supply lines from Germany, and attack the Nazis from the rear. We would make a vise—we the eastern side, the D-day army the western side—to crush them."

Henry nodded again. It was a simple but brilliant way to sandwich the Nazis and squeeze.

"So we prepared. We made an airstrip in Vassieux to receive four thousand Allied and French paratroopers that de Gaulle promised to send to help us fight. In June, the BBC broadcast the order: *Les montagnards doivent continuer à gravir les cimes*. The mountaineers must continue to climb the heights."

The doctor paused, closing his eyes, as if listening to the radio once again. "So we closed the passes. We raised our flag. We attacked Nazi convoys and patrols. But the plan's success, our survival, depended entirely on the paratroopers coming. Our *maquis* were excellent fighters, but they only numbered a few hundred. All we had were peasants, horse carts, and whatever guns we could steal. And courage, of course, a legion of courage and *esprit de corps*."

Henry noticed the doctor's hands had begun to tremble.

"All through France, underground Resistance newspapers celebrated our bravery, using us to inspire other Frenchmen to rise up. Despite this, no paratroopers came. We were left to face the Nazis alone."

Henry felt sick. He knew just how the SS and the Gestapo would react to such defiance. "Nothing? The Allies sent nothing? Are you certain your radio signals got through?"

"Oh, they got through." Anger crackled through the doctor's voice. "For weeks, de Gaulle's headquarters radioed back, telling us to hold on a few more days, that there were weather delays, that the paratroopers might be needed elsewhere, Eisenhower's forces were pinned down at Normandy, that our airstrip needed a few more yards of length before they could use it. London did parachute in Sten guns and Enfield rifles. Oh, yes, and machine guns from World War *One*. The guns jammed the first time they were fired—by eight farmers trying to hold back three hundred German soldiers armed with tank mortar that blasted holes in mountain rock.

"We also begged the Allies to bomb the Nazi airfield in Chabeuil."

"Wait," Henry interrupted. "I came past that airfield. I saw destroyed Junkers. We must have bombed it."

"Your Allies claimed their air reconnaissance showed only ten planes. Therefore, the field was not a 'credible threat' worth risking fliers and aircraft. What about the risk to our villagers, our children? We radioed back that our spies knew the Nazis had hidden sixty planes in the forest. Finally, the Americans were sent to fly a raid. But they hit the wrong field, miles away. When they did hit Chabeuil, it was already too late."

Henry hung his head. He knew how orders were often messed up when transmitted from the French through the British to the Americans. Crews could be sent to bomb the wrong sites and then redeployed the next day to correct the mistake, needlessly risking their lives twice. The fliers had a word for it: *snafu—situation normal all fouled up.*

He persisted in trying to find something positive. "But we dropped personnel. When I was here last spring, there were SOE men, British special ops, experts in explosives and espionage. Right?"

"Yes, they sent SOE. The British also dropped engineering officers to guide the airstrip construction and "pianists," radio operators. The American OSS parachuted in fifteen rangers led by two young lieutenants from South Carolina and Texas we could barely understand." The doctor tied off the coil of bandages around Henry's chest with an irritated yank that made Henry gasp. "Brave men but not exactly the four thousand paratroopers we expected."

The doctor's bitter sarcasm grew. "But of course, we are grateful for the great patriotic display on Bastille Day, July Fourteenth. In broad daylight, seventy-two Flying Fortresses roared over Vassieux, escorted by fighters from Algiers. We rejoiced, thinking, finally, the paratroopers had come. But it was more arms and food containers, eight hundred of them, floating to earth on red, blue, or white parachutes. The planes circled and then roared away.

"Those canisters barely hit the ground before the Luftwaffe flew in from Chabeuil, alerted by the sound of all those engines, the sight of all those chutes. Villagers tried to cut loose the containers, to salvage what they could. They were gunned down. Within days, ten thousand German troops invaded our little mountain citadel."

Henry couldn't believe it, desperately didn't *want* to believe it. Flying Fortresses were B-17s, American bombers. How could headquarters be that stupid—that many planes in broad daylight was like painting a big red arrow in the sky. "But didn't de Gaulle back you? He was your leader. His Free French Army was just across the Mediterranean in Algeria. He could have flown in reinforcements within a few hours. Did he know what was happening?"

The doctor glanced nervously to the square outside the church, where his "boss" was sitting, hunched, staring off into space, holding a cup of barley coffee he wasn't drinking. "Oh yes, de Gaulle's headquarters knew. *Le patron* radioed for an immediate air bombardment, saying if they did not at least do that, they were criminals and cowards."

He lowered his voice. "Some believe de Gaulle's people betrayed us. What is the American phrase? Hmmm—'*Sold us out*.' Correct?"

Henry nodded.

"We may have been nothing more than a diversion, a way to distract the Nazis while the Allies battled in Normandy.

"We know now that there were many French paratroopers in Sicily awaiting orders. They were so frustrated at sitting, doing nothing, they nicknamed themselves *les paratouristes*. It seems de Gaulle and his senior staff planned to use them elsewhere, while praising our courage through radio broadcasts. I believe they were already thinking politically rather than militarily."

"I am sorry, doctor, I don't understand what you mean."

The doctor narrowed his eyes. "After the humiliation of our long occupation, de Gaulle wanted France to feel strong again, to look like the French were freeing France, not just helping the American and British do so. He was saving those paratroopers for a drop into the Massif Central, in the middle of France, where it would be easier to make it into Paris with the Americans and British."

He leaned forward. "Some speculate that de Gaulle doesn't want communists and socialists in his new government, even though he needed us to liberate France. *Le patron* is a socialist. Many of us here are communists." He shrugged. "Interpret it as you will."

Henry was stunned. The Allies hadn't even completely won the war yet—how could the French already be fighting amongst themselves?

The doctor tilted Henry's head toward the light to look at his forehead, which was still oozing blood from *le patron*'s blow. "This will heal on its own. It looks as if it was stitched up recently."

Henry blushed. He definitely didn't want to admit to the shenanigans of that late-night flight of his. "My mother sewed me up after an accident on the farm."

"I could use her here," the doctor murmured.

"Don't you have a nurse to help you?"

The doctor's face darkened. "No. No longer. We hid

wounded *maquis* in a cave, Grotte de la Luire. But *les boches* found us. They slit the throats of the wounded and let them slowly gag to death. The seven women who helped tend them were deported to Ravensbruck. The other doctors and our hospital priest were executed by firing squad. I escaped into the cavern's underground passageways with a patient. We waited three days before coming out." He closed up his bag with a snap. "I am not proud of it."

He turned to go. Henry caught his arm. "What happened to the villagers?"

"What happened?" the doctor croaked, his face haggard. "After that *parachutage*, the Germans dropped incendiary bombs on our towns. They strafed anyone running from the fires. They used our airfield—that de Gaulle's staff had claimed was too short—to land gliders, carrying SS with orders to exterminate.

"Exterminate." The doctor half-sobbed the word. "They slaughtered two hundred people around Vassieux alone, old men, children, women. They castrated men, raped women, gouged out eyes, cut out tongues.

"There was a twelve-year-old girl buried under rubble, who pleaded for help and water for days. The Nazis laughed at her and shot any survivor who tried to approach to save her. Finally Father Gagnol"—he nodded toward the soft-handed man—"convinced them to let him dig her out. He brought her to the hospital. But it was too late. She died."

The doctor ripped his arm away from Henry's grip. *"Patron,"* he cried, "I am done here."

CHAPTER ELEVEN

Henry sat dazed, horrified, incapable of absorbing it all, because to do so, he would have to comprehend it. How could anyone understand such savage behavior?

He had seen friends mangled by flak. He'd survived Luftwaffe pilots trying to blast him to bits. He'd endured being tortured physically and psychologically by the Gestapo. Becoming the object of that kind of calculated cruelty, like a mouse toyed with by a cat, changed a man—and not for the better. But it was nothing compared to what the doctor described, that kind of sadistic annihilation of an entire valley of people.

How could anyone go on after witnessing that?

Henry watched *le patron* ease himself up off the bench, square his shoulders, and turn to come into the church. The priest shadowed him, protective.

That was how. One step in front of the other. Breathe in. Breathe out. Remember the kindness, the bravery that managed to flicker amid such darkness. Like Pierre. Keep faith in that capacity within humans and follow the beacon up out of the abyss. One step in front of the other—a slow march back.

If this grizzled *maquisard* could keep walking after such devastation, Henry sure could, too.

Henry rose, straightened his spine to ease the bite of his rib, and extended his hand to shake the old warrior's. They were compatriots of a sort—waging war against their own internal demons of regret as surely as they had fought real battles against the Nazis. Henry understood why *le patron* hit him, the lunacy of it. Perhaps he was suffering flashbacks, too, and he saw Henry as the personification of those who had betrayed "his children." Sometimes crazy actions carried their own logic. After all, Henry had stolen a plane to talk to God in a midnight sky. It'd made complete sense to him at the time.

Henry wasn't going to expect an apology from the old fighter. He'd make it all right for the guy. *Le patron* had known enough humiliation.

As Henry grasped *le patron*'s hand and smiled reassuringly, he could see a quiet gratitude in *le patron*'s deep-set, droopy eyes. Recognizing it, Henry felt some of his own turmoil fall away.

Maybe it took a broken rib for him to begin to mend.

"Henry Forester, sir. Second lieutenant, American Air Forces."

Le patron nodded in greeting and gestured to the pale-faced man. "This is Father Gagnol."

It was the first time Henry really had a good look at the priest. He caught his breath. It was Pierre's priest. He was certain of it.

"Father. Boy, am I glad to see you!" Henry was so excited he got all tangled as he blurted out why. "You're just the person I'm looking for. Well, not the person, but the person who can help me find the person."

The priest shook his head. "Slow, my son. My English is not that fast."

How could he be slow now? Henry wanted to jump up and down like he had when he was little and trying to grab Lilly's attention. "I've come back to find Pierre."

"Who?"

"Pierre!"

"There are . . . were . . . many Pierres here, lieutenant."

Henry took a deep breath to make himself coherent. "Right. Of course. Let me explain. Last year, end of May, maybe the very first of June, I'm not sure exactly of the date, I brought a little boy to you. Your *maquis* was moving me. The Milice had arrested Pierre's mother and shot his grandfather. Pierre was eight years old. I gave him my good-luck marble. You said you knew monks who would protect him."

"Ahhhhh." The priest finally brightened. "I know this boy. Pierre Dubois." He paused, thinking. "I did not take him myself. The Milice were here that week, led by that informer." He looked to *le patron*. "That devil-woman collaborator, 'Colonel' Maude."

Le patron scowled. "The one who made Monsieur Bellier sit down naked in a red-hot frying pan."

The priest nodded, blinking back tears that had welled up in his eyes.

Le patron put a large, strong hand on the priest's shoulder. "You saved twelve from execution that day, *mon ami*. Your pleas moved monsters."

With surprise, Henry looked more carefully at the pale, gentle priest. He remembered his instinctive distrust of him when they'd met the previous year, prejudiced by Clayton's dismissal of anyone who didn't do work outdoors or with his own hands. Well, it took a lot of spine to argue with Nazis. Henry's time on the run had certainly taught him that courage came in all sizes, ages, and gender of people. This journey was teaching him that courage was needed to fight internal battles as well.

He bit his lip to wait a few beats out of respect for the

homage *le patron* was paying Father Gagnol. Then he tried again. "About Pierre, sir. Do you remember where you sent him?"

"Yes. We were cut off from the abbey I sent children to before. A thousand Nazis were between us by then. So I sent him with a guide to a monastery north of Grenoble. Far away to be safe. I do not know if he made it. Trouble came to us soon after. I have not thought of him." He crossed himself. "I will remember him in my prayers from now on."

"You have no idea what has become of him?"

"No. I have buried two hundred of my flock. I lost track of one boy." The priest spoke angrily, and then waved a hand in apology. "*Pardonnez-moi.*"

"What about his uncle Jacques?"

Father Gagnol turned to *le patron*. "He was part of the Forêt de Lente *maquis.*"

Le patron shook his head. "Dead."

"What about the *maquisard* who led me that night?" Henry pushed on.

"I do not remember who that was, lieutenant."

"He was a kid, maybe sixteen? I didn't know his name. Pierre was the only one who told his name. Oh, wait. Maybe this will help. He was a musician, a trumpet player, from Paris. His parents had been deported."

The priest stopped him. "Yes, I know Yves. His father

85

was a half Jew, so he was sent here to hide. Yves had a beautiful voice. He sang for my church."

"That's right! We sang a Louis Armstrong song! He had a great set of pipes. I owe him a record. I promised I'd . . ." Henry stopped. He could tell from the priest's face. The musical teenager was dead.

Henry hung his head, remembering walking down the mountains with the boy, singing, pretending to play trumpets like Armstrong. And their final parting, when Henry asked to know where to send the record album.

"How will I find you?"

"Vivant, j'espère."

Alive, he hoped.

This time Henry fell silent and *le patron* prodded. "What is it that you want? What will you do if you find this Pierre?"

All this time, Henry hadn't really thought through that. Until this morning he had hoped—despite all the dire news—to find Pierre safe and sound, his little farm operating happily somehow, his mother making that wonderful fritter of potato and onion. Having now heard the full story of the Vercors's obliteration, Henry knew his first job was to find Pierre and then help him find whatever was left of his family. With some foreboding, he asked, "Pierre's uncle thought the mother was shipped to Ravensbruck.

Could she have survived?"

More and more, *le patron* answered for the two French-men. The priest looked relieved at seeing the old *maquisard* revive. "A few Ravensbruck prisoners—*celebrities*—were exchanged," he began. "De Gaulle's sister was one. But we have no word of the camp. We hope the . . ." He paused, and nodded slightly, as if reminding himself of something good about the Allies. "We hope the Americans liberate it. Last week, your General Patton reached Buchenwald. His troops care for the prisoners until they are strong to travel. We look for rooms in houses that are left for those who may come home to us."

Henry mulled over the situation. "I don't think there is anything else for me to do really but go to that monastery. If Pierre is there, I can look after him until we know what has happened to his mother."

"We can care for the child, lieutenant," said the priest.

"No! I want to do it," Henry spoke sharply, and then blushed for it. "He saved my life. He hid me for a month. I am pretty sure the Milice arrested his mother because of me." He looked at *le patron*. "It's important that I make that right somehow." He paused and added, his voice hoarse, "I promised Pierre that I would be with him in trouble. Unlike the paratroopers, *monsieur*, I've come."

The old *maquisard* crossed his arms across his broad chest and scrutinized Henry. Henry returned the hard gaze. Slowly, *le patron* smiled. Henry could tell that once upon a time that smile had led to hearty laughter.

"Then we gather charcoal for my gazogène car. I drive you. The monks may not be helpful." *Le patron* clapped the priest on the back. "Pardon, Father. You are the only man of the cloth I trust. You and *le Barbu*. Remember what *le Barbu* said when he joined us? He said, 'I kill Germans with my cross and then read the funeral mass over them.' A priest to my liking."

Le patron picked up his walking stick, adding for Henry's benefit, "We socialists do not like the Church." He strode off, shouting over his shoulder, "Come. *Vite.*"

Chapter Twelve

Henry sat on smooth gray leather in the backseat of a Citröen *deux chevaux*—a trophy stolen from the Germans in Grenoble during a nighttime raid for medical supplies. *Le patron*'s men had risked the heist because a British SOE officer had landed in a tree when he was parachuted in and broken his arm. The doctor had needed plaster to set it and there had been none left in the Vercors villages.

"As they leave the hospital, they see the commandant car outside a certain mademoiselle's apartment, keys inside. *Voilà.* I ride in style." *Le patron* was driving and talking, gesturing with both hands to make his points. More than once Henry had gasped and braced himself, as *le patron* turned to look at him during the telling of a story and swerved wildly, nearly hurling them off the narrow high cliff roads.

Le patron must have been making the other man in the car nervous as well, because when they stopped to dump more charcoal into the burner, that man took over the wheel. The new driver was from Senegal, a huge, six-foot-three expanse of man with wide shoulders and a long neck. He had a devil of a time folding his lanky legs up underneath the steering wheel of the sleek, small car. To fit under the roof, he'd taken off his fez, a tasseled red pillbox hat left over from his French colonial uniform. He, too, had been a trophy of a kind, a prisoner stolen from the Germans.

"That was our best raid," said *le patron*, describing how his *maquis* freed fifty-two Senegalese POWs. He was so desperate for trained soldiers because of de Gaulle's failure to send the promised paratroopers, *le patron* allowed a dangerous raid to Lyon, about sixty miles northeast, a city controlled by Gestapo.

"*Les boches* had the Senegalese waiting tables in their officers' mess. Such a use for such fine fighters. Our contact told us they did not sleep near the Aryan Nazis, because they were black African. They were housed down the street and went to work by bus."

From the hit-and-run raids Henry had seen the French do, he knew that bus ride left the Nazis open to an ambush—something the *maquis* were masters of.

"The drive there—*très dangereux*. At checkpoints our

fighters pretend to present papers. They slam on the accelerator to crash the barricades. If chance holds, we run over *les boches, aussi.* The kidnap? Simple—as if our Senegalese brothers knew our plan. Our trucks surround bus. They disarm the guard and jump in. *Pouf! Cinq minutes, c'est fini.*

"*Le Barbu* was on that raid. A fine man." *Le patron* paused. "At least he died fighting." He became silent, looking out over a gorge to a long series of ridges, the stark white rock furrowed into eerie, looming shapes, like broken tusks.

Henry was sorry he hadn't met the "the bearded" priest. The Friar Tuck–like minister evidently had arrived in the Vercors along with a Russian deserter and a sauce chef from the famous Maxim's restaurant in Paris—all drawn by the growing reputation of the brave little Resistance band in the mountaintops. Henry marveled at the hodge-podge of people willing to risk so much.

"How far to the monastery, *monsieur?*"

"Hmmmm. *Une heure.* The monks live in seclusion. First they must answer the gate. I bring my friend to persuade"—he patted the Senegalese's arm—"because I lose patience with the Catholic order. Some priests and nuns helped the Resistance, but many Church officials supported the Vichy and the deportation of Jews and political 'undesirables.' When we begin our republic anew, we must separate religion and government." Grudgingly he added, "Like your country."

He gazed out the window a little while longer before turning around in his seat. "I admire your President Roosevelt. He saw your country starve and used the government to make jobs, to stop *l'avidité* . . . hmmm. Greed, *oui?* In businesses."

Henry thought of how Clayton had hated those subsidies, FDR's public works programs, and farm quotas to control crop prices. "Handouts for the lily-livered," Clayton had snarled. "I take care of my own." Not everybody had Clayton's spit, though, that kind of mean strength. Henry wondered if Clayton's opinions about "government interference" would change if he witnessed what Henry was now seeing in France.

He turned his focus back to *le patron*, who was still designing a new France: "The state must control coal mines, trains, canals, and factories to make sure all Frenchmen receive the same. We must pay workers fairly. To rebuild we must work as one, not laborers for the rich. Roosevelt understands this, *oui?* I read about him—a great thinker. He will help de Gaulle see this?"

Henry realized that *le patron* didn't know about FDR's death. "I'm sorry, *monsieur*. President Roosevelt is dead."

The *maquisard*'s face fell. *"Zut!"* He slammed his hand

against the back of the car seat, startling the Senegalese driver. *"Le seul Américain qui vàlait quelque chose est mort!"* he said, telling the driver that the only worthwhile American was dead. "That leaves only Stalin to help France control de Gaulle."

Henry was shocked. The Allies' wartime alliance with the Soviet Union was an uneasy one. To most Americans, the Red leader was as bad as Hitler. Stalin and Soviet communism held an iron fist of repression over the Russians. There was no freedom there. Soviet social equality simply meant one of equal suffering.

It was beginning to feel like liberation was only turning the world upside down instead of righting it.

"Regardez." As the car descended a sharp slope of primroses and butterflies, *le patron* pointed to a huge, glistening lake. Jutting out onto it was a flowering peninsula with a little white rectangular castle. It had pretty pointed slate roofs, courtyards, and geometric gardens within its walls.

Henry peered out the window. "Wow. Who lives there?"

"The monks."

"In something that fancy? I thought monasteries were about giving up the good life to pray," Henry couldn't help wondering aloud.

"Hmpf." *Le patron* snorted. *"Exactement."*

Well, thought Henry, they certainly should have been able to feed Pierre decently.

The Senegalese banged hard on the door of the gate. Ten agonizing minutes passed before a robed monk appeared and asked with a down-turned head what they wanted. Henry's heart pounded so loud in anticipation and hope that he couldn't hear what the monk was saying, his voice muffled by his hood.

Le patron was getting agitated as he listened. Henry's sense of foreboding grew. When the monk closed the gate, the *maquis* leader shook his walking stick at it and paced back and forth, threatening to come back with some plastique to blow up the wall.

Henry didn't need to translate *le patron*'s tirade. Pierre was not there and perhaps had even been turned away. Henry picked up a rock to hurl into the lake, sending a slice of pain through his ribs. He crouched to catch his breath, to contain his panic.

Only the Senegalese kept his head. He noticed several nuns laboring up the road, carrying baskets heavy with wild strawberries. They almost ran away as the African dashed up to them. But when he bent himself over in a large ceremonial bow, they stopped. Watching, Henry rose. *Le patron* grew still as well.

After a few moments, the African came back. *Le patron*

translated as his Senegalese companion explained, the two languages overlapping each other. *Trois enfants.* The sisters had taken in three children. *Deux filles.* Two girls brought to them by their governess when their parents were deported. The teacher had returned recently to take them into her home.

Et le troisième? And the third?

The Senegalese glanced at Henry. *Un petit garçon.* "*Il s'appelle Pierre.*"

Henry caught his breath with joy. *Where? Where is he?* Why the heck was the African soldier being so slow to tell him? Why did he look sad?

In a torrent of words Henry could not understand, the man explained more. Henry couldn't wait for the translation. He grabbed the Senegalese by his blue jacket. "Where? Where is he?"

Gently, *le patron* pulled Henry off. "Gone, lieutenant. Run away. A month past. They know not where. He spoke very little, so no clues. We would know if he had returned to the Vercors. He is lost."

NO! Henry's search was not over just because he'd run into a dead end. He rifled through the conversations he'd had with Pierre, searching for any mention of family other than that in the Vercors. There was none. Where would he go? Henry gazed along the lake, thinking, trying to imagine the mind-set of a brave but distraught child. If he were Pierre, where would he go?

Wait a minute. The lake itself seemed to provide an answer for Henry, at least a place for him to continue his search for Pierre. Last year, as he came out of Switzerland, a lake and a wise woman had sent him on his way home. Could Madame Gaulloise somehow still be alive? *Le patron* had said prominent women had been released in prisoner exchanges. Maybe she had been, too. Of all the people in the world, she was the one he could trust most to help him think through the possibilities of where Pierre might have gone. If the Gestapo had sent her to prison, it would have been Ravensbruck. Maybe she met Pierre's mother there. Maybe.

Henry had nothing else to go on. "How far is Annecy from here, *monsieur*?"

"Annecy? Hmmm. *Trente kilomètres.*" He pointed up the road.

Thirty kilometers. That would be about eighteen miles, Henry reckoned. No problem.

"*Pourquoi?*"

"There is a lady there who might be able to help me."

"I do not have charcoal to travel there and return to my people."

"That's all right. I can walk. North up this road?"

"*Oui.*"

Henry shouldered his bag, wincing. But it would be all

right. The bandages kept his ribs tight. It probably was just bad bruising. Besides, a cracked rib would heal as long as he didn't hit it again.

Le patron noticed Henry's grimace and grimaced himself. "I am sorry, lieutenant."

Henry took his hand to shake good-bye. "It is all right, *monsieur*. *Pas du tout*. I have war wounds, too. *Je comprends*."

"Ah, *oui*." Once more, *le patron* studied Henry's face. "What then shall we do?"

"Pardon me?"

"You know not your catechism? When John the Baptist preached the coming of Christ, he told the people they must change. The people asked, 'What then shall we do?' And John answered, that the person with two coats must give one to him who had none; and likewise with food. It is from the gospel of Luke. You make me think of it."

Henry was surprised. "I thought you did not like the Church, *monsieur*."

"The Church, *oui*. I did not say that I did not have faith." *Le patron* smiled. "There is work to do. You remind me of that. *Merci*."

He kissed Henry on both cheeks—a strange gesture for such a gnarled and brusque man. But Henry knew it to be the highest tribute. He gave his. He stepped back and saluted. *"Au revoir, patron."*

Le patron and the Senegalese warrior climbed into the German commandant's car and headed south. Henry turned northward and once again set off on a French road, not knowing what he would find at the end of it, a stubborn hope his only compass.

CHAPTER THIRTEEN

In the heart of Annecy, Henry stood by a canal threading its way through the city. Just as the lake was cradled within mountains that rose sharply from its shores, the canal was framed tightly by rose and gray-green stucco buildings. Pots of geraniums, hanging from wrought iron balconies and bridges, reflected as red dots in the still waters as the entire street replicated itself upside down in the blue mirror. Moored boats floated in water and clouds. Here and there snow-white swans drifted by, asleep, heads bent under wings. Henry was amazed they hadn't been stuffed for Sunday dinner. Annecy's aura was so peaceful, so intact compared to the destruction of Vassieux. Maybe Madame was all right after all.

Henry had never really made it into Annecy before. He'd hidden in Madame's elegant house on its edge. But he remembered that the canal linked the lake with a river. Her walled mansion was by a river. So he followed the canal. Along the waters came the sound of conversation, laughter, dickering. He began to see people with baskets, filled with fish or handfuls of rutabagas or onions.

"Il y a des oeufs à vendre!" A man trotted by Henry and shouted across the canal to a friend that there were eggs for sale.

The friend started jogging a parallel route. *"Et quoi d'autre? Tu sais?"*

"Des cerises!"

"Superbe!" The man darted across a bridge to join the other and the two continued to lope down the street.

Eggs for sale. And cherries. Henry followed.

Around a bend the small street opened into a square jammed with people and carts. Nothing was in abundance, but the townsfolk seemed ecstatic that any food was for sale. Henry couldn't get near the egg vendor, so many crowded him. But he did approach a woman selling milk from huge tin jugs. Her donkey cart was pulled by a massive dog. It looked mighty antsy harnessed up, clearly unused to the job. There was no way Speed would stand still for pulling that thing, thought Henry. He wondered what might have happened to her pony—confiscated, eaten?

"Combien?" Henry asked how much for a cup.

"Avez-vous votre carte de rationnement?" she asked.

Henry had no ration card.

The woman shrugged. *"Tant pis."* Tough luck.

Henry looked over at a wagon with knots of dark flat bread and started for it.

"Vous ne pouvez pas acheter du pain si vous n'avez pas une carte de rationnement." The woman stopped him, saying he'd need a ration card for the bread as well. She looked him up and down coldly, assessing.

Henry tried to gauge what she was thinking. She was slim, angular, her skin sallow, but with ten more pounds on her she'd be rather pretty. He couldn't tell her age exactly, but she was probably not much older than he was. It was her slightly cunning expression that aged her.

In a lowered voice, she offered to sell him a ration card for bread for 150 francs. Henry wondered how she'd come by it. Was it stolen, or counterfeited? How much trouble could he get into for using it if he were caught?

His stomach growled loud enough for her to hear. She smirked. Henry tried to decide if he should spend the equivalent of three dollars for the card. He'd have to pay more for the bread itself. He'd already eaten three cans of Spam, taking him down to nine. He better save them for days he was crossing open country. *"D'accord,"* he agreed, explaining he only had American dollars.

The woman's eyebrows shot up. For a moment a desperate eagerness crossed her face before she adopted a nonchalant disinterest. She could not change American money, she said, what did he take her for, a bank?

Henry began to see the game. The smallest bill he had on him was a fiver. That would take him down to $191. As he considered, he noticed the dog's ribs, her toe tapping nervously. What was he going to do, chintz a girl who obviously had lost her farm horse, whose dog was skin and bones, and who was that worked up about the idea of five bucks? His good heart got the better of him.

Henry pulled out his five dollar bill and looked over at the bread cart again. The loaves looked dry and hard. He'd sure love a cup of that milk. Would she give him a cup for a pack of Camels?

Again, the girl's eyes widened momentarily at his offer. Then she veiled them, looking down, pretending it was a big imposition on her, but she could see he was hungry, so out of pity she'd take the cigarettes. When she gave him the tin cup and took the cigarettes and money, her hands trembled.

Henry sat down on his bag with the milk and the tiny loaf. The milk tasted slightly sour, but he needed it to get the barley bread down. When he handed the cup back to the girl and strode off, he heard her snigger and say to the bread girl what a fool he was. She would have given him all the milk for one pack of Camels. She planned to make eighty francs off each individual cigarette.

Henry kicked himself. The sea captain had said that he could live off those Camels for a month if he were smart about it. Well, he'd better wise up, hadn't he, if he expected to eat in France.

"Monsieur?"

A boy about Pierre's size and age stopped him. He held a long flat basket laden with big, gorgeous cherries for sale. *"Vous voulez acheter des cerises? Une poignée pour quinze francs?"*

Fifteen francs for a handful of cherries. That was only thirty cents. Henry did have two quarters in his pocket. And a half pack of gum. The boy looked so hopeful. Henry's resolve to be more money savvy instantly faltered—this boy reminded him too much of Pierre. Henry would just be more careful about his money tomorrow.

He asked the boy if he would take fifty cents, American. He handed him the gum, a gift.

The boy grinned, delighted. *"Pour moi?"* he asked.

Henry nodded and asked in muddled French if he needed a ration card for the cherries.

The boy shook his head. Most fruits and vegetables were not rationed, just meat and eggs, and bread, and milk, and wine, and sugar, and paper, and leather, and coal, and . . . The boy trailed off, perhaps realizing that it was easier to say what was *not* rationed.

He wrapped a handful of the deep red fruit in a scrap of newspaper.

Henry was about to ask the boy where he lived when a woman fluttered up in great excitement over the cherries. She must have heard Henry talking with the boy and spoke to him in English. "Excuse me, sir. I must see the year's first cherries." She was well dressed, but like them all, thin and pale. A flush of happiness lit up her face as she surveyed the fruit. *"Mon Dieu. Elles sont belles."* She patted the boy's face, telling him that his farm must be doing well, that he brought her hope for a better season, of France blooming again.

The boy beamed back. *"Oui, madame, elles sont excellentes cette année."*

She purchased two handfuls, the boy heaping them. Henry was startled to see tears on her cheeks as she gently balanced the cherries. She turned to him, with a smile that was both embarrassed and jubilant. "Today, my son's name is on the list of released prisoners. He is coming home. I will make a *clafoutis* for him with them. It is his favorite. He loves cherries, since he was a boy."

She tiptoed away as if any jostle might bruise the precious fruit. "My son is coming home," she said to anyone she encountered. "My son."

People parted to let her pass.

*   *   *

Watching, Henry's throat tightened. He remembered Lilly's face when she saw him standing in their driveway, alive; Madame Gaulloise's voice when she spoke of her own son in a Nazi POW camp; Pierre's mother explaining why she risked her life to work in the *maquis*—for her son's freedom.

Then he recalled crawling over the wall to Claudette's orchard, when he was starving—what a gift the cherries growing there had seemed.

Ever so carefully, instead of eating them himself, Henry tucked the cherries into his coat to save for Madame Gaulloise and her son in case they somehow had survived.

He continued on.

CHAPTER FOURTEEN

"Elle n'a aucune nouvelle de ta soeur?"

"Non."

Two middle-aged women turned a corner and passed Henry. One held a sprig of purple lilac and looked as if she had just received a death notice. Henry could translate that she was worried about her sister. She pulled out a handkerchief, dropping the lilac.

The other picked up the blossom and held it as her friend blew her nose, loudly. She asked about a Madame Rousseau and a photo.

"Oui, oui, j' la lui ai montrée." The woman began to sob, saying she had shown her sister's photo to Madame. But Madame knew nothing about her.

Something about the name *Rousseau* made Henry stop, stoop to tie his shoes, and eavesdrop. Henry had carried a novel by Jean-Jacques Rousseau in the train station to signal Madame Gaulloise that he was "her package." Clearly Gaulloise was a code name for her, since it was a brand of French cigarettes. Could Madame Gaulloise and this Madame Rousseau the women were discussing be one and the same? It was a ridiculous long shot, he knew. But he'd been grasping at straws since coming to France.

After a few moments the distraught woman was collected enough to explain more of what Madame Rousseau had said to her. Henry could make out *Ravensbruck, 45,000 women prisoners, slave labor*. And that Madame had given her the lilac as a symbol of hope.

The two women fell silent. Finally, the friend put her arm around the distraught one's shoulders. *"Alors, on n'a plus qu'attendre et prier."* Together, they went to wait and to pray.

Ravensbruck. Henry hurried to the corner and peered down the street the women had traveled. It quickly opened into countryside. In the distance were the glistening waters of a river. Beside it was a gracious manor house, plumes of purple cresting over its garden walls.

Henry caught his breath. He recognized it. It was Madame Gaulloise's house. And if he understood the women right, she was there—alive!

Henry bolted down the street and banged on Madame Gaulloise's door. Giddy with relief, he wondered if the butler would recognize him.

No one answered.

He banged some more. His knocking boomed in a hollow echo.

Still nothing. No footsteps, no yapping from Madame's little poodle.

Henry backed down the stairs, realizing that the marble horse heads that once had flanked their bottom rung were gone, knocked off their pedestals. He tried to catch the bottom ledge of a first floor window, to pull himself up to look inside, but they were just out of his reach. He did note, though, that the lavish curtains he remembered being in the parlor, framing the windows, were missing.

Uneasy, Henry walked the perimeter of the house and the wall to the river side of the estate. He heard the creaking of a gate drifting *open, shut, open, shut* in the gentle breeze off the water. He followed the sound.

Puffs of wind brushed the ivy around, revealing a tall door leading into the garden. Henry put his hand on the sun-warmed wood, held his breath, and pushed.

The first thing that hit him was the wonderful fragrance of lilac, of spring. The garden was overgrown, blooming wildly with wisteria and tulips. In the far corner, basking in the sun beside a forest of the purple lilac, was a small woman. She faced away from Henry and was wrapped in blankets, her head and neck covered in scarves as colorful as the garden surrounding her.

Just like Madame to take in an invalid, thought Henry. The house was probably full of refugees she was helping, just as in the year before. She must be upstairs tending to them. That's why she hadn't answered the door. Barely able to contain his excitement, he called out, *"Pardonnez-moi, est Madame Gaulloise ici?"*

The woman did not respond. Henry approached, repeating his question about Madame's whereabouts as he came around to face her.

Henry halted, aghast. The woman was so bundled in blankets, he couldn't tell how thin she was, but her face was skeletal, all eyes it seemed—huge, dark, mournful eyes.

"Eh, barre-toi!" A tall young man appeared from inside the house and tried to shoo off Henry. *"Elle a déjà répondu à assez de questions comme ça aujourd'hui."*

The youth was bone thin but vital, about Henry's age and size. He was shouting that there had been enough questions for one day. He had to be Madame's son.

Too excited to be polite, Henry blurted out: "I am looking for your mother. She saved my life."

"Ahhhh." A small voice, as whispery as the garden's scents, came from the blanketed woman. *"Chéri.* Now I recognize you."

The invalid, the living scarecrow, was Madame Gaulloise.

★ ★ ★

Henry followed the son through Madame's house, just as he had once followed her butler. Madame had insisted that Henry spend the night. The son, suspicious, hostile, had led him to a guest room with no comment. Henry excused the silence. His mother was in the shape she was because of him and other Allied fliers.

With each step through her home, Henry's anger and disgust grew. The Nazis had taken most of her furniture and books, urinated in zigzags to stain the rose-silk wallpaper, and cut out the eyes of the portrait paintings. They had left the baby-grand piano, but had carved "Jewlover" along its top and snapped some of its strings. Henry remembered the night Madame Gaulloise had played that piano for him, pieces by Beethoven, Chopin, and Debussy, she'd said. He'd developed a terrible schoolboy crush on her, completely beguiled by her intellect, her matter-of-fact courage, her beauty.

Back downstairs, Henry tried to picture her as she had been a year ago, as her son carried her inside, laid her gently on the one remaining sofa, and propped her up on pillows. A little cloud of down feathers puffed out of gashes left by the Nazis.

"So, *chéri*, you made it home," she said, settling in, a twinge of that vivacious smile lighting her emaciated face. "Your *maman* rejoiced, yes?"

Henry nodded. He was fighting to find his normal voice, he was so appalled by her condition. Madame had taken his hand when he came into the room. Hers was so frail, the light shone through her skin.

Henry told her of his homecoming, of Lilly, of Patsy, of Clayton throwing two baskets of eggs into the air because he was so glad and surprised to see Henry alive. He joked that he had been so thin when he got back that Speed had been the only one to recognize him at first.

Madame actually laughed, a tiny throaty burble. "So, you were much changed, as am I, *chéri.*"

Her son looked away sharply and swallowed hard. Henry took a deep breath to steady his own emotion. "But you are still beautiful, Madame. *Très belle.*"

Those dark, sad eyes brightened. "A compliment? You have become bolder, young man. But I fear your French pronunciation is still . . . hmmmm . . . well, now you have time to work on it." She self-consciously straightened the scarf around her throat and touched the one on her head, to make sure it was in place. Both were festooned with delicate orchid patterns, a swirl of rich mauves and lavenders.

Henry could see that all that was left of her dark, glossy hair were little tufts. Sores scarred her temples. He had to force himself to smile.

Madame studied Henry a little longer.

"Aha!" She glanced over at her son and said, "You see, darling, I am remembering more and more. This young man wanted to take a scarf like my Hermès home to his *maman*. He loves her dearly, just as you do me. Having such a son live, such a son come home, makes all of this right. *S'il te plaît, ne pleure pas.* Do not mourn."

Henry could see the son's jaw clench as he ground his teeth.

Madame turned back to Henry. "You were number thirty-seven."

Thirty-seven! Henry knew well that each person she helped raised her risk of exposure. "How many did you save, Madame?"

"Forty-six," Madame answered proudly. "I am afraid the last flier did me in."

The son muttered some French oaths and moved to the window.

"It was my own fault, darling." She tried to quiet him. To Henry she explained: "The Nazis were becoming more watchful, more clever. They purposefully stepped on the toes of train passengers to see what they might exclaim. A Brit muttered "bloody hell" and they got him. What linked him to me was a foolishness on my part."

Henry was ahead of her. The Rousseau book. He remembered it was set in Montreux, where Madame had picked him up, her stop on his ratline to freedom. If her real last name was indeed Rousseau and the Nazi who got the guy had been one of the officers Madame had charmed for petrol or at the gaming tables, the link would be easy to make.

She nodded and threw her hands up. "And the greatest foolishness was my name *is* Heloise, just like the title." She shrugged. "Perhaps I was tempting fate, trying to show just how stupid the Nazis were by waving my real identity in such a way right before them. Hubris, *non*? Pride. Since the Greeks, since *Oedipus*, it has been the tragic flaw that brings down our heroes and ends the play." She smiled, then faded, worn out by talking.

Henry and her son watched her for a few minutes, to see if she might drift off to sleep. But she didn't. Madame remained awake, watchful but withdrawn, beyond their reach, like a small animal that backed itself into a hole to watch a predator pace right outside. Henry remembered that feeling, trying to stay on alert but shut down at the same time, because any flicker of emotion would catch their attention, spur the Gestapo on, ignite their cruelty.

Henry felt sick with sadness. Seeing that wary look, how ingrained it was in Madame, told him more than anything what she had endured. He was completely lost as to what to say. This woman had been strong, fierce, like Joan of Arc, a crusader. And now . . . Henry glanced at the son and cringed at the anger on his face. He knew how he'd feel if he ever saw Lilly so reduced.

A few awkward minutes dragged past. Henry couldn't stand not doing anything to try to help. He searched his mind for some sort of solution. But what could possibly address such damage? Then Henry remembered something simple—how wildflowers, hatched robin's eggs, and other beautiful things of nature had always cheered Lilly when Clayton was being difficult.

Triumphantly, he pulled from his pocket the cherries he had purchased from the boy. "I have brought these for you, Madame. A boy was selling them in the market."

Madame gasped. *"Des cerises!"* She struggled to sit up and reached for one. Thrilled to see her so revived, Henry held them toward her.

"Stop!" The son lunged and grabbed his mother's wrist.

Crying out in pain, she collapsed and nursed her arm. She was so delicate, even that gentle of a knock left her bruised.

Her son knelt beside her, slamming his hand against the floor in self-loathing. *"Pardonne-moi, maman."*

"Please," she whispered, her eyes welling up with tears. *"S'il te plaît, est-ce que je pourrais en prendre une? Une seule?* Just one?"

"Non, maman."

Crushed by her son refusing, she pleaded to Henry, "Please, young man. Please, may I have one? I have not tasted any fruit since they arrested me. Please?" She seemed almost frantic.

Henry was bewildered, furious. Why the heck couldn't she have some of the cherries? She was clearly starved and desperate to have one. "Of course, Madame, they are for you," Henry extended his cupped hand again.

"*Idiot!*" The son shoved Henry back so hard and suddenly the cherries scattered across the floor. "They could poison her. Americans have killed hundreds of deportees that they liberated from the camps by giving them candy bars and C-rations. The prisoners' stomachs, so shrunken, were not ready. After all they survived, food killed them!

"She can have nothing but gruel in teaspoonfuls right now." He choked on the words. "Nothing more." He caught his mother's butterfly-delicate hand and kissed it tenderly. "*Je suis vraiment désolé, maman.* Remember what the doctor said. You must trust me. You must."

Madame looked at him with such disappointment, such weary acceptance of being denied food. She seemed to wither in front of them. But she managed to touch her son's face lovingly and whisper that she understood. "*Je comprends, mon petit.*"

Then came the cough.

It was a tiny gag at first. Then rattling heaves that shook her body. And finally violent retching that left splatters of blood on the handkerchief her son hurriedly held to her lips. She reeled in breath with a scraping rasp, the same kind of agonizing clawing for air Henry had had trying to survive the bathtub torture by the Gestapo.

For a moment she calmed. Then the cough began again.

"Get out!" The son shouted at Henry. He held his mother, rocking her gently. "Breathe, *maman*. *Respire pour moi.*"

Henry backed his way out and hurried for the garden, for light, for air. A cough like that could only mean one thing—tuberculosis, a killer disease that consumed the lungs until someone could no longer breathe. Madame was dying.

CHAPTER FIFTEEN

That evening, the son found Henry in the garden. Henry was doing the only thing he could think to do for Madame. He was weeding her flower bed.

He'd made quick work of it—a childhood of hoeing and picking was worth something at least. He'd uncovered a wide swath of little white blossoms, dangling from their stalks like tiny bells. No longer choked by the coarse grasses that Henry had yanked and piled up, their fragrance burst into the air. It reminded him of the perfume Madame wore when he had first met her. He'd picked one to sniff more carefully and was sitting cross-legged in the gravel walkway when Madame's son approached.

"What are you doing?"

Henry jumped up, embarrassed to be found smelling flowers. "Just thought I'd tidy up your garden a bit."

The son looked distracted, or perhaps perplexed. Clearly he'd never dirtied his hand with thinning out weeds.

Henry tried to strike up a conversation. "I was wondering," he said, holding up the delicate spray of white blossom, "what these are called. I've never seen them before."

At first the son seemed startled by the question. "Lilies of the valley," he replied. He looked out toward the river. "Next week, on May First, there is an old tradition in Paris. People leave the city to pick lilies of the valley in the forests. We give them as good luck. I wonder if anyone will remember to do it. Who can remember flowers now?" He paused, rubbed his forehead, and then murmured, "Mother and I did it every year when I was small."

Lilies of the valley. Henry heard his own mother's voice waft to him, singing,

> "White coral bells upon a slender stalk,
> lilies of the valley near my garden walk.
> Oh, don't you wish that you could hear them ring?
> That will happen only when the faeries sing."

Lilly believed in faeries and the magic of flowers she'd never seen. Such delight in what the world did offer had kept her strong, hopeful even during the Depression and in a difficult marriage. Henry had realized last year, when he finally made it home, how Clayton's toughness had groomed Henry to be resilient, to survive the war. Now he recognized how Lilly's influence had kept his spirit alive as well.

Both young men stood awkwardly, deep in thought.

Finally, Madame's son seemed to shake himself. "My mother reminds me to show my manners." He smiled for the first time. "And to apologize for being rude. She is correct. After five years in a German POW camp, I forget the niceties of life. My name is François Rousseau." He extended his hand and bowed slightly.

Henry took it. "Henry Forester." Hoping to establish some kind of friendship, he said, "Moms are like that. I survived missions over Germany and being hunted by the Nazis and my ma still reminds me to wipe my boots on the mat when I come in."

François laughed. "My mother wishes to speak with you. She is in the parlor. I will prepare dinner." He smiled again, sheepishly. Henry was beginning to see touches of Madame's face in his. "It will not be good, I am afraid. We have very little and I am only learning now to cook. Our cook was arrested with our butler."

"Will they return soon?"

François's smile vanished. "They were shot for helping my mother protect airmen. They made Mother watch. That seems to be the only thing that she truly regrets about all this—their execution. Somehow she believes her time in prison, her ruined health, is all worth it to save boys like you."

François took a step toward Henry and grabbed the collar of his jacket. The gesture was not threatening, but urgent. "Be worth her sacrifice."

He released Henry's coat and walked into the house. The words dealt Henry a blow as hard as the *maquisard's* to his ribs. Madame had saved forty-six lives. What could he possibly accomplish that would be an adequate counterweight to the loss of this brave woman? Him, with his nightmares and high-strung nerves.

Slowly, purposefully, Henry filled himself up again with a long, deep breath. He straightened his back, steeling himself by the bite at his bruised rib. "No kidding, Forester. No more sniveling. Get it together. From now on. You owe Madame that at least."

Inside, Madame was sitting at the piano. A paisley shawl covered her shoulders, but now it was painfully clear just how thin she was. A good wind would blow her away, thought Henry. Her arms and fingers were all bones. And yet, as before, those long fingers were pulling out beautiful music from the piano. A serene, lilting melody floated above sustained chords, like shifts in dappled sunlight atop a pool of water. Once again, Henry felt himself inching toward her to listen.

The pinkie of her left hand touched a key that thumped dead, her thumb a key that jangled wire. Madame sighed and stopped. "Such cretins." She shifted her hands to play the piece up an octave, where the Nazis had not cut the piano's strings. "*Voilà*. Here they cannot touch me."

Madame played on, peaceful content smoothing her face. The music closed on a whisper, a slow resolution of dissonance to a chord like the ones that ended hymns at Henry's church. She froze as the held harmony throbbed and dissolved into the air.

Only then did Madame look up at Henry. "*C'est très beau, n'est-ce pas?*"

Henry nodded. "What was that, Madame?"

"Mendelssohn's 'Consolation' from *Songs Without Words*. It is hard to understand how a nation that spawned him, Beethoven, Brahms, Schumann, can listen to Hitler. How a people who make such music can exterminate an entire race of people. Angels and devils in the same soul."

Gently, she reached to touch Henry's hand. "Now, *mon ami*, why are you here? I sent you home. As glad as I am to see you, you disappoint me."

Henry quavered. Her concern was such an invitation to spill his soul. But he stopped himself. He could not burden her, in this depleted state, with his nightmares, the wild actions that had driven him back to France. He'd reclaimed that much self-control and recognition at least. So he told her about Pierre, about Pierre's mother. "Her brother said they would send her to Ravensbruck. Do you think she survived?"

Madame's face clouded. "Do you know her name?"

Henry only knew the boy's first name. Wait—the priest had said Pierre Dubois. Did she know a Dubois in her late twenties, very pretty, dark eyes, petite in size? What an idiot he'd been not to learn her first name.

Madame smiled sadly and shook her head. That description fit hundreds. "If she is young, hopefully she was strong. She would have to be strong. Every several weeks we all had to lift our skirts to our hips and run in front of the SS guards and doctors. Women who were too weak to run, or were slow, or had swollen feet or legs, were pulled aside to be transported to Mittweida. The guards said there was a place for them to recover. In truth they were gassed to death in the transport trucks."

Henry thought he would vomit. "I am so sorry, Madame. I feel like this is my fault." Henry poured out the story of the Gestapo's interrogation, of the SS officer holding up a scarf and saying they held a woman they suspected had aided him, of his managing to kill the Nazi and escape.

Madame stopped him. "Then, you see, *chéri*. Your escaping the Gestapo did save me." Her smile was incredibly generous, like a Madonna's in the paintings that had once graced her house along with the jumbled up Picasso. Henry remembered her talking of her romance with the painter and how, on the day that he left, the Picasso was gone—sold to finance his escape. Henry owed this woman so much. And she was still trying to help him. "The worst part was Herr Barbie, in Lyon," she continued. "He told me he was going to hang me with an American they had just picked up. Then he never mentioned it again—which was a small victory that buoyed me with hope. It clearly was you. Since you were clever enough to escape, they could not use you against me. *Merci, mon chevalier*. Once I arrived in Ravensbruck, it was not so bad."

Henry felt a wave of redemption that somehow his actions may have helped her even a little. But he wasn't so sure that Ravensbruck was "not so bad." "You lie to make me feel better, Madame."

"Oh, only a little lie, *chéri*," she teased. "You call them 'white lies' do you not? Such an odd expression. Why white? White is pure. It should be gray, or pink perhaps, tinged only slightly with the red of deception. I have never understood the metaphors of English. It is a hard language to grasp. Oh, and *mon Dieu*, your Americanisms. *Pff*!" For a moment, Madame was once again the witty woman who fliers would follow anywhere, completely trusting in her clever courage and put-on drama.

Then she sobered. "But it was English that saved me in

the camp. My knowledge of German, French, and English. There were so many nationalities—Poles, Russians, German Jews, Dutch, gypsies, captured SOE agents— they used me as a translator. So I avoided the worst labor. Other women had to pull huge iron rollers to pave streets, dig ditches and canals to drain the marshes, clear forests. Each day, twelve hours of backbreaking work. They could not do that for long on what we were fed—a half pint of brown water they called coffee, one pint of beet soup, and a fist-sized hunk of bread. That was all for the day. We tried to survive on dandelions we could pick through the barbed wire, by drinking water we drained off their truck engines when the guards weren't looking. We salivated over the single sausage we were granted once a week. But for most it was not enough. Many dropped dead as they labored, and were left to rot.

"Better that death, perhaps, than the experiments. That was the worst thing I had to do, to explain their plans to infect women with bacteria, to sever their nerves, to break their bones to see how or if they would heal. To translate the lie that if the prisoners agreed to such tests or to be sterilized, they would be freed. I tried to warn them, I tried." Madame gagged and held her hand to her mouth.

"Don't, Madame. Don't try to tell me any more."

She was trembling. "No." Her voice was hoarse. "You must hear. You must tell your countrymen. Already people do not want to acknowledge, cannot face what was done. But they must if we are to prevent it from happening again. The horror of it will keep us vigilant."

"You are a remarkable woman, Madame. I don't know how you survived."

Madame closed her eyes and ran her fingers along the tops of the piano keys. "I remembered this," she whispered. "I remembered my son's laughter. I recited poetry I knew by heart. I refused to weep. Those who cried at night were dead the next morning.

"I built a safe fortress with my memories, an inner peace that came from knowing that I had done what had to be done." She opened her eyes and looked at Henry, a flicker of energy left in them. "Camus wrote that man's grandeur lies in his decision to rise above his condition. 'There is no fate that cannot be surmounted with scorn.' Do you know his writing?"

Henry did not.

"Hmmm. You must. Look on my shelf. See if you find *Le Mythe de Sisyphe*. Perhaps the Nazis left that. Yes, is that it?" Henry was holding up a thin volume. "Take that with you."

"It's in French, Madame."

"*C'est vrai*. It will improve your French skills. You will have plenty of time to work through it on the train to Paris. It is merely a long essay. Camus is important for you to know. He was in the Resistance, editor of the underground paper *Combat*. The next to last line of this book is most inspiring: 'The struggle itself toward the heights is enough to fill a man's heart.'" She nodded to herself. "'The struggle itself.' *Oui.*" Madame drifted off in thought.

"Wait," Henry was focused on something else she'd said, not on the literature. "A train to Paris, Madame?"

"*Oui.* I suspect that is where you will find your Pierre—at the station where the liberated prisoners return. Thousands will come through in the next few weeks and months. I was released early, one of almost three hundred women the Nazis selected to be exchanged for German prisoners de Gaulle held in France. I was selected because my Swiss friends had continued to protest my arrest. We were thought to be the most presentable, the least damaged, to soften the reality of the camps. I suppose we were—only eleven of us died during the train trip.

"I do not think people awaiting us knew what was to come. They held lilacs and lipsticks and face powder to give us, thinking we'd merely be tired from a long journey and want to freshen up. They did not know that our hair had been shaved like sheep to make yarn for sweaters, that we were covered with lice and sores, that our teeth were rotted, that we were consumed with dysentery, TB. A man asked one of my friends, who could barely stand, where her luggage was. Imagine! She handed him all she had, a black sweater tied in a bundle to protect belongings she had counted over and over again. I can recite the contents after hearing it so often—two safety pins, a ball of twine, a shard of soap, a button, one aspirin tablet, a pencil nub, a comb, a match. These were treasures in camp.

"We sang 'The Marseillaise' as we stepped off that train. Such off-key joy we had. But the crowd could not join us, they wept so in shock at us."

She quieted. Henry could barely hear her final instructions. "At the station, I saw children holding signs with their names written on them, hoping their mothers would step off the train and see them. Or that one of us would know something of their parents' fate. *Pauvres enfants.* Look there. At Gare de l'Est. Or at Hotel Lutetia, where the returnees go if no one awaits them at the station."

Henry caught her as she swayed and almost toppled off the piano bench. Gently he lifted her. She didn't weigh more than a couple bags of feed. As he settled her on the sofa, François came in with a tray—soup for Henry and a tiny portion of thin, oatmeal-like gruel for Madame.

Gratefully, Henry tasted his vegetable soup. Madame's stories of her deprivation had made him hungry. François was right. He wasn't a very good cook. But Henry was happy to not be eating Spam for one night anyway.

François pulled up a footstool to sit in front of his mother, intently watching as she lifted the spoon. She looked so resigned, uninterested. Henry was sure if the soup was poor, the gruel was terrible. So he was surprised to see her reaction as she slipped the teaspoon past her cracked lips. Madame brightened and flushed. She rolled that mouthful around and around before swallowing.

Her son beamed.

"I tasted that little bit of cherry, my darling." Even though painfully soft and low, her voice was playful, like she was sharing a secret. "It tasted like . . . like . . . a miracle. Like seeing you—a miracle."

"I remembered that if I begged hard enough that you would give me cake for breakfast sometimes, Mother. How could I refuse you the season's first cherries? *Je t'aime, Maman.* Now, there are two cherries in this bowl. Cut up very small. But you must eat all this gruel to have them." François said the last in a singsongy voice parents used to coax children to take medicine.

Madame responded with a tiny chortle that resonated in the room as beautifully as the piano music had. Her son was radiant. All over a few teaspoons of gruel and a thimbleful of cherries.

Henry tiptoed out.

The next morning, early, as the sun was just beginning to reach over the garden walls to warm the sanctuary inside, Henry finished weeding. He'd been out since five A.M. or so, awakened earlier by the sound of violent coughing, doors opening and shutting, someone knocking loudly on the front door, feet running up the stairs. Something had happened.

Weeding kept his dread in check.

When he was completely done, he plucked a lily of the valley to press into the Camus book. He wanted Lilly to see what her song was about. He flipped the pages. The writing was short, but in highfalutin French. It would take some doing for him to puzzle it out. But Madame thought he should, so he would.

François found him. "Henri, come here."

He looked exhausted. Henry approached him warily.

François pressed one of Madame's delicate scarves into Henry's hand. It was a deep forest green, etched with ferns and flowers. Henry recognized it as the one she had worn when he had pretended to be her chauffeur.

"Oh, no," Henry shook his head. "She has given me way too much already." He tried to give it back.

François closed Henry's hands around the beautiful silk. "I insist. She wanted you to have this. To take home to your *maman*."

Want*ed*? Henry tried to push away the word's implication, the feeling of a chord of music resonating and then fading away. He forced cheeriness: "I am going to follow her advice and go to Paris. May I say good-bye to her?"

But François's face told him before he said it. Madame Gaulloise was dead.

CHAPTER SIXTEEN

On the train to Paris, Henry ached. The hurt spread from his heart, through his breathing, to every inch of his being. Madame's mischievous delight in outwitting the Nazis had made her seem invincible. But war wasn't a game, was it? No one—not even the bravest, the most resilient, the most clever and idealistic—was untouchable. Henry tried to cling to the fact that the Nazis had not sullied Madame's spirit—that had remained indestructible.

François's plea that Henry make himself worthy of Madame's sacrifice hounded him. Clearly, the beginning of answering that tall order was to snap-to. *"Straighten up and fly right,"* as the Nat King Cole song went. *"Cool down, papa, don't you blow your top."*

That and to find Pierre. If Pierre's mother were in the same shape as Madame, he would desperately need

Henry's help. Saving that small life would have made Madame happy, Henry knew. And at least that might be a small counterweight to the heft of her loss.

Without hesitation, Henry shelled out twenty-five dollars for the train ticket. He had to hurry. He couldn't waste a week hiking or hoping to hitch a ride. Every day trains pulled into Paris that could carry Pierre's mother or the news that she was dead. Henry's heart told him that Paris was where Pierre would be, waiting, looking, if he were . . . Henry shut down that thought before his mind could whisper the doubt that Pierre was alive.

Henry refused to do the math of his finances or worry about the cost of a Paris hotel. At least he had nine days of Spam left. Right now he was just living day by day, making things up as he went along. There wasn't any flight plan for this journey.

To distract himself, Henry pulled out Madame's book. It was short—only four chapters—but hard going. He'd never before read much French literature. His teacher, Miss Dixon, had given him a copy of *Le Petit Prince* when she learned he had joined up to be a pilot. She'd said it would be good luck for her "prize French student," since a little prince from a faraway asteroid guarded a pilot who crash-landed in the Sahara Desert. Henry had muddled through it, translating a sentence or two per page so that he got the gist of the story. The watercolor illustrations helped, he had to admit. After reading it, though, Henry had left it at home, feeling that a book about a pilot going down, even to crash-land safely, was *bad* luck.

Le Petit Prince had been poetic and simple. This book by Camus was dense and philosophical. Still, Henry managed to understand that Camus felt life was absurd and meaningless and that hoping for a better tomorrow only made it more so. Science and logic could not explain the world. Henry agreed with that. But, gee whiz, how depressing could you get? He closed the book and stuffed it back into his bag.

Blasting whistles told him that the train would soon pull into Lyon. Henry shifted in his seat, cramped by the bodies packed in the enclosed riding compartment. His knees touched the man's sitting opposite, and he was sandwiched between two older, very round, country women. The man and the women seemed to know one another and gossiped nonstop. Henry drifted in time, their voices swirling around him, as he listened to the memory of Madame playing the piano.

It was the smell that stopped his daydreaming. A horrible smell. *What the heck was that?*

Henry sniffed, wrinkling his nose in disgust. He looked around the compartment, to the lady to his left, the one to his right, the man across, wondering if they could smell what he did. They looked back. Their faces seemed to carry a sudden, put-on innocence. Like the look he and his friends had masked themselves with when one of them hit their peevish seventh-grade teacher in the back of the head with a spitball.

Henry took another good whiff and fought off a gag. It almost smelled like Mr. Campbell's barn back home when he slaughtered pigs for market.

The smell came from above. He glanced up at the suitcase rack over the window, scanning the pile of hat-boxes, cardboard suitcases, and carpetbags. Was he see-ing straight? One of those bags had a dark red splotch in its bottom corner. As Henry studied it—*jeepers!*—a large drop of blood oozed out of it and slid down the wall.

Henry jumped up. "Do you see that?" He pointed.

Everyone in the car looked at him blankly.

"Aw, come on, people. Don't you see that? Don't you smell it? It's blood. *Du sang.*" Henry's mind reeled. Given all that he'd heard about in the past few days, he imagined a chopped-up body inside the tapestry bag.

When Henry reached for it, the man across from him stood and slapped his arm away, telling him to keep his hands off. *"Sinon on va penser que vous êtes un voleur."*

"Thief? I'm no thief, mister. What's in there?"

The man glanced nervously at his companions. Henry realized everyone else in the compartment was in on whatever was concealed in the bag. The situation felt like

a scene in a Hitchcock suspense film, where the one character who wasn't in the know was quickly disposed of or
framed to seem the insane one. Well, that wasn't going to
happen to him.

Henry lunged for the bag. But the man knocked him
back to the bench. One of the women grabbed his arm.
She held her finger to her lips. "Shhhhhh."

Shush? You've gotta be kidding! Henry was about to shout
out, when the compartment's glass and wooden door
swooshed open. The conductor entered, accompanied by
two French policemen, one short and pudgy, the other tall
and muscular.

"Hey! Over here!" Henry pointed to the blood, but the
policemen were way ahead of him, as if they knew exactly
what to look for and where. One pulled down the bag and
opened it. Henry held his breath to look, half expecting
to see a decapitated head. Massive shanks of lamb were
inside, pooled in blood, recently butchered. The other
officer undid the hatboxes to reveal stacked wheels of
cheese.

"Des porteurs de valise," the police muttered and
nodded. Henry's compartment-mates were black marketers, "suitcase-bearers." The policemen prodded
them and Henry with thick sticks. *"Vous êtes tous en état
d'arrestation. Venez avec nous!"*

"Wait, you can't arrest me," Henry said. He pushed

back, prompting the brawny policeman to grab him up under his armpit, lifting him to his toes. "Listen, I had nothing to do with this. I don't know these people. I was just sitting here."

"*Ah, oui?* Open your bag for inspection." The portly policeman switched to English.

"Gladly." Henry untied his duffel bag, without thinking about its contents. Out spilled his SPAM, his cigarettes, and the ration card for bread.

Henry felt his face turn red, then ashen. "I can explain those," he started.

"No need." The fat policeman smirked. "These"—he pointed to the Spam and Camels—"U.S. soldiers steal from their army to sell to our people, exploiting our hunger." He pushed the ration card with his stick. "As an American, this you could only have if you are in the company of black marketers. You are under arrest, *monsieur*. Come along."

"No, wait, you don't understand. I've got to get to Paris."

"Paris? You go to jail, *monsieur*. Then we will call your army's military police to send you back to the United States. We do not want your kind in France."

Chapter Seventeen

Chink-chink. Chink-chink.

The jailer rattled a large ring of keys as he passed Henry's cell. He stopped at the next cell to lecture the "suitcase-bearers" on their *crise morale*. If it were up to him, he jeered, peasants trying to become princes by selling their wares through the black market would be hanged. One of the women started to cry.

Chink-chink. Chink-chink. The policeman walked on, pausing at the next cell to ridicule an old man who was serving eight days for picking his neighbor's carrots because he was hungry, then two teenagers jailed for having a fistfight over a precious box of matches. The prisoners swore at him, then became silent.

"Jerk," Henry muttered, "having fun taunting these poor people."

The jailer had labeled Henry a *"sal Américain."* It'd twisted Henry up inside. How could a Frenchman call him "filthy" with the same tone in which he'd heard the *maquis* curse the Nazis?

If the French saw him that way, what would the American police, the MPs, do with him? Henry had seen MPs break up enough fights in the base canteen to know they didn't stop to ask questions. If they believed that he was a black marketer, the least they would do is send him home, without his finding Pierre, without his getting himself right for Patsy—a complete disaster.

The Army might even throw in jail time for behavior unbecoming to an officer. Was he still subject to that? Henry concocted a dozen defenses about why he was in France. Somehow he just couldn't see the MPs buying that he was looking for Pierre. From the sounds of it, too many American soldiers had tried to turn a profit off French misery. His stash of American canned food and cigarettes and the counterfeit bread card certainly suggested Henry was in the game as well.

Henry rubbed his forehead along the bars of his cell, trying to squash his growing sense of failure and the memory of the last time he'd been in a French prison cell, waiting— when his French guide had turned him over to the Nazis, who in turn hurled him into an unlit, windowless cellar in a prison-chateau. That dark cage had been his introduction to the brutal manipulation of a Gestapo interrogation. The hours in utter darkness were designed to rattle him so he entered questioning already vulnerable with fear born of his own imagining of what was to come. "It's not the Gestapo, it's not," Henry mumbled to himself once again, desperately trying to push back the curtain of memory closing him in, shutting out the light of present day.

But his mind betrayed him and threw Henry back into pitch-black dark, into the Nazi hole:

Six feet by five feet. Henry's fingertips ran along the dank, dirt walls as he counted the room's perimeter.

Ten hours. Maybe a day since the Gestapo locked the door. Henry couldn't keep time straight in complete darkness.

Pray for me, Ma. God listens to you. Pray that I will be brave. Pray that I won't tell anything to save my own skin.

Screams from the next room. Footsteps. A door groaning open. Blinding light.

"Your turn, American."

"Stop it, Forester," Henry berated himself aloud. "It's not happening. Feel this." He wrapped his fingers around the bars of his cell. "Bars, not a dirt wall." He crammed other voices into his head to replace the Nazis' to pull himself out of the flashback. Think of what other people have survived and carried with them as they managed to walk, Forester, one foot in front of the other, like the Vercors's *patron*, like Madame, like François. "Listen to them," he ordered himself. "Be worth Madame's sacrifice. You have work to do."

As painful as the thoughts were, Henry made himself hear Captain Dan and the conversation they'd had the morning of their last flight, when Henry had preflight jitters: *Don't get flak-happy on me, Hank. You're the steadiest copilot I've ever seen.*

I'm with you, Captain.

Dan's confidence in him had made Henry feel strong, like someone Dan could trust. Henry could be that person again. It would be like flying a raid: Grit your teeth and focus on getting to the target; don't be distracted by things blowing up all around you.

Henry steeled himself, as he had countless times before takeoff, his mind free of the cloud cover of its own torment, prepped for flight. Locate Pierre, help him, and get back home—mission accomplished.

Come back to me, Henry. Patsy's voice—sweet, beckoning—called to him.

I'll find a way, Pats. I will.

Henry shoved the Gestapo back into the dark and waited for the MPs.

* * *

"This him?"

Two huge men in khaki, combat boots, and the telltale armbands and white helmets marked MP stood in front of Henry's cell.

"*Oui*, this is the scoundrel."

"Let's go, soldier."

"I'm not a soldier anymore," Henry answered.

"Yeah, yeah, save it for our CO." The MP waggled his thumb toward the exit.

Henry stepped out of the jail cell. "I need my gear."

"Right."

At the door, the fat French policeman handed Henry's bag over the counter. As the Frenchman lifted it, his blue coat swung open. Henry spied an unopened pack of Camels in the *gendarme's* breast pocket. *Hey now!* Henry started to open his bag right there, to confirm his suspicions that the guy who arrested him for black-marketing had stolen the very things that had gotten Henry in trouble. But the MPs hustled him along.

In the jeep, Henry confirmed it—all his Spam, the cigarettes, and the bread card were gone. He was now down to $145 and he had no food backup or bartering items. He scrambled through his things again, looking for Madame's scarf. He'd be sick if they'd taken that. His fingers grasped silk. He kept digging to find the Camus book. There, too. *Thank goodness.* Madame's gifts had become as important to him as that good-luck marble had been on his bombing raids.

The jeep jolted along Lyon's cobblestone streets, the MP driving quickly. Sadly, Henry noted the irony that his quest to find and help Pierre, the child warrior of the Resistance, would end in a city that had been a center of *maquis* uprising and a Gestapo stronghold to squash it. *Hold on a minute.* If the French had stolen Henry's things, there was no evidence left to use against him. Henry sat back in his seat, working to contain his excitement, centering himself with the sound of Dan's voice. *Steady. You're not completely clear of the flak yet, Hank.*

Henry had never mastered a real poker face. The boys on his crew could always call his bluff during cards. Now was the time for Henry to stop being a naïve farmboy, so trusting, so open, so easy to read. He would just have to figure out how to mask his thoughts and play the fact of the missing items at the right moment, in the right way. It was the only trump he had.

Ready, Hank? Keep sharp for bogeys.

Ready, sir.

CHAPTER EIGHTEEN

The military police headquarters was busy—lots of people in and out, soldiers arrested, soldiers released, soldiers just hanging about. The MPs plopped Henry into a row of chairs in the main hallway and went to a desk to check him in. For a moment, Henry considered bolting out the door and into the street, but he knew he'd make it about twenty yards before he was caught. Besides, that would blow his game—his story that they didn't have anything on him. Henry stretched out his legs and yawned, pretending boredom.

The hallway was full of American civilians on some sort of official business. They all seemed to wear the same round glasses, tweed suits with wide lapels, and baggy pants. They stuck their thumbs in the pockets of their waistcoats or smoked pipes—intellectual-looking men

who appeared as uncomfortable in their attempts at non-
chalance and lounging as Henry felt.

One among them caught Henry's notice. He was a tall,
broad-shouldered blond, whose golden hair was parted
severely and slicked back. About him hung an air of arro-
gance—something about the way he crossed his arms and
surveyed people down his fine, chiseled nose, something
about his staccato voice. British maybe, or just oddly harsh
the way he pronounced words. Most voices sounded harsh
to Henry after growing up around Tidewater drawls, but
there was something about this one that disturbed him.
Mesmerized, Henry kept watching the man. What was it
about the guy that sent Henry into fire drill mode?

The blond man met Henry's gaze. Henry gasped a bit
at his eyes. They were a deep, bright blue against the man's
pale skin, blue like cornflowers. Henry couldn't stop staring at them. Where had he seen blue like that before? Blue
like the rim of a flame everyone thought was the coolest
part of a fire, but in actuality was the hottest, most scorch-
ing element—the part that could melt flesh off bone.
Those eyes.

Then the man laughed at something his companion
said, a sneering, guttural snort. It was like a firecracker
going off by Henry's ear.

This time Henry couldn't stop the memory. He was
back in the Gestapo cell, arms tied, soaking wet. He had

just been yanked up out of a tub of water and was gagging for breath, for life. Two men held him while the Gestapo torturer in charge spoke: *We will give you the count of ten, American. Ten seconds of air. Ten seconds to tell me the name of your Resistance contacts.*

Eins, zwei . . .

No? Oh, too bad.

The men holding him laughed, one in a sneering, guttural snort.

. . . 8, 9, 10.

The man on his left arm lowered his face to Henry's, eye-to-eye. *Ready, American? Ready to die for your country of mongrels?*

Eye-to-eye!

Henry knew exactly where he'd seen that blue before, where he'd heard that snide laughter, that cold voice.

Hatred threw Henry from the chair onto the blond man, knocking him against the wall and both of them to the floor. "Bastard!" Henry screamed. "You Nazi bastard!"

He slugged that contemptuous face, pummeled it until the MPs came running and jerked him up and off. But Henry had bloodied him. Bloodied him good. It'd be a long time before those blue eyes could see straight to hurt someone again.

"Get off me!" Henry kicked and flailed. "He's a Nazi, part of the Gestapo. He tortured me. Arrest him, not me!

What's the matter with you? Look on his arm for the tattoo they all had. He's SS!"

But the MPs dragged Henry down the hall, threw him into a room, and locked him in.

When the door opened, it wasn't an MP or Army officer who stepped in. It was a heavyset, round-faced American with thick-rimmed glasses, followed by a guard who stayed against the wall. He waved Henry to a seat and lowered his own bulk into an armchair. He pressed his fingertips together before saying, "Well, son, you've gotten yourself into some trouble."

Somehow "son" didn't sound friendly. Henry remained silent.

"Trafficking in stolen American goods and counterfeit ration cards. Attacking a civilian."

"That was no civilian, sir. I know that guy. Boy, do I ever know him. He's Nazi SS." For once Henry knew exactly what was real and what wasn't during one of those nightmare memories. That flashback brought him clarity, not fog; strength, not fear. "I'm telling you, he is a Gestapo torturer. He near drowned me in their bathtub of persuasion. It happened farther down toward the border with Spain. My guide ratted me and a couple other fliers out to the border patrol. And they gave me over to the SS. For two days that SOB helped interrogate me. I'd recognize those eyes and that voice anywhere."

The man pursed his lips and thought a moment. Then he snapped his fingers at the guard, who left the room, once again locking the door.

What kind of weird game is this? Henry forced himself to wait, to hold his thoughts close to his chest.

"Let's start over." The man turned chummy. He offered Henry a cigarette. Henry declined, careful not to add that he didn't smoke, which would have made his having so many cigarettes even more suspicious. He wondered if that had been the point of the offer—to trip him up.

"My name is Thurman. Who are you exactly? And what are you doing here?"

Henry told his name, his rank, his record, how he went home, how he came back across the Atlantic taking care of cows and horses.

"But what are you doing in France?"

Henry used serviceman back talk. "Who wants to know?"

"The United States government, son. Don't play the stud with me. You're in enough trouble as it is. I can put you in the brig of a troopship heading back to the States this afternoon on charges that'll land you in jail for a couple of months. A U.S. Army court-martial just sentenced a GI to life imprisonment for selling twenty gallons of gas on the black market. The Army takes this seriously. Did you come over here thinking you'd make a few bucks?"

"No, sir." *Lord, a life sentence.* But Henry forced calm. *"Cool down, papa, don't you blow your top."* He copped a what's-the-big-deal attitude and explained about Pierre. That his mother had packed the Spam, that the ship captain had given him the cigarettes. So what?

"Where'd you get the bread card? The French are pretty hot about our guys messing around in the black market."

Here was his moment. Henry took a deep breath. "What ration card, sir? Has anybody shown you this ration card they supposedly took off me?"

Thurman sat back in his chair and smiled slightly. "Nope. No one seems to have any of the things they said they found on you. No hard evidence." He paused a moment. "You were with the Resistance?"

"Yes, sir. They saved my life."

"How long?"

"Couple of months, sir."

"Any of them Reds?"

"Sir?"

"Communists?"

Henry knew some of the *maquis* were communists and socialists, just like *le patron* was. But Henry didn't trust this guy at all. For sure, he'd spent the war driving a desk. Henry shrugged. "Not that I remember, sir. What does that matter?"

"Could matter a lot if Stalin decides he wants to keep on marching right through Berlin into France. Because of the Resistance, the *Parti communiste français* is well organized and armed. It does not like de Gaulle. The members are very adept at organizing worker strikes that could paralyze the country. We believe it takes orders directly from Stalin and his politburo."

"We?"

Thurman looked Henry over carefully for a long moment. Then he pulled out a business card and handed it to him. It read: Office of Strategic Services. "Know what we are, son?"

Whatever they were messing around with now, OSS agents had risked torture and death to help the Air Force be clearer on targets. "I know you guys sent agents behind lines, like the British SOE did, to gather strategic info. And that your counterintelligence corps tried to screw up the Germans with false leaks."

Thurman smiled, pleased. "You could be a help to us, son, with your knowledge of the French Underground. Give us a call when you get back to the States." He started to get up.

"I'm not going back to the States anytime soon, sir."

"Ah, yes, you are. I can't let you off scot-free. I can let the French charges drop because I don't have the evidence in hand. But we can't have Americans just strolling around France right now.

"Unless, of course"—he paused and leaned forward—"you can supply me with information that could help us keep France free of Reds. Some of these communist groups are working hard to build anti-American feeling. A newspaper came out yesterday claiming that when we bombed Hitler's factories in France we were really just trying to weaken France so that we could take over its market with U.S. products after the war—economic imperialism, they called it. That's a line straight from the Soviet Union propaganda machine. I bet you could give us a list of some Resistance people we should keep an eye on until we know they really are with us. A little friendly surveillance, that's all. If you could do that, I could look the other way about your being here."

Thurman let that sink in for a few seconds before adding, "We're just trying to put Humpty Dumpty back together again in France, son. We want to make sure he looks more like Uncle Sam than the Russian Bear when we finish."

Henry frowned. Snitch on the political leanings of people who'd risked their lives to save him? He remembered what the Vercors doctor had said about de Gaulle's dislike of socialists and communists. The whole thing stank.

Well, Henry was learning fast. Two could play at this not-so-subtle game of blackmail and bribe. He hardened his voice. "What are you doing with that Nazi?"

"What Nazi?"

"Look, Mr. Thurman. I don't know what you're doing here. But I can tell you that guy I hit in the hallway is Gestapo. Maybe you think he can help you track communists, because the Gestapo was so ruthless hunting down the *maquis*. Or maybe you think you can use him to rat out other, higher-ranking Nazi SS hiding in France or on the run back to Germany. But that guy tortured Americans like me. He should answer for it. And God knows how many French he killed."

Henry leaned forward himself, so close to Thurman that he could catch the whiff of real coffee on his breath. "Bet my friends the French policemen would be interested to know that Nazi is walking around 'scot-free,' as you put it. I don't think they'd cotton to the idea of his hanging around with you when you obviously know exactly what he is—an SS torturer."

Thurman glared at Henry.

Henry glared back, refusing to blink.

Suddenly Thurman burst out laughing. "Be sure to call that office when you do go home, Forester. I like you. I could use a guy like you." He stood up and extended his hand. Slowly Henry rose and took it. Thurman's hand was clammy. "Where in France did you say you were heading next?"

"Paris, sir."

"I'll see if I can arrange a ride for you with our

supply trucks heading there. A favor between friends, eh?" Thurman walked out the door, leaving it open.

Friends? No way. He and Thurman just negotiated a mutual blackmail. Henry wouldn't divulge that Thurman was protecting a Gestapo torturer, and in exchange Thurman wouldn't send Henry back home or alert American authorities that he was in France. That was no friendship.

Henry wiped his hand on his pants leg to clear it of sweat-slime. But he wasn't going to ever be able to wipe himself completely clean of the deal he'd just cut, would he? How many fliers had that Nazi drowned or beaten to death? Would it be worth the exchange of helping Pierre—saving one young life by letting the murderer of many go?

Chapter Nineteen

"Ever been to Paris?"

Henry sat in the passenger bench of a large U.S. Army supply truck next to a young private. A sergeant was driving and a long convoy stretched out behind them.

"No, I haven't," Henry answered. Despite his sorrow and worries, he was excited to see "the city of lights." He wondered if the Louvre would be open. He had never been in a museum before. Patsy loved to draw and was forever checking out library books about painters. She'd told Henry that a portrait of a woman by Leonardo da Vinci called the *Mona Lisa* was at the Louvre. *Mona Lisa*'s eyes would follow him around the room, she'd said. Henry would sure like to see that painting so he could tell Patsy if the woman's eyes really were that magical, to show he'd been thinking of her in France. Was she thinking of him? he wondered.

"Don't expect too much," grumbled the driver.

"Excuse me?" Henry asked, startled. Could this guy know what he was thinking about?

"Don't expect too much from Paris," the driver repeated irritably. "It's overrated."

"Ah, come on, Sarge, it's the most beautiful place I've ever seen," said the private, who smiled at Henry. He was from Oklahoma and his openness reminded Henry of wide fields and clean breezes. "Notre Dame, the Eiffel Tower, the Seine . . ."

"Yeah, the Seine," barked the sergeant. "It stinks. It's full of garbage. They relieve themselves in *pissoirs* on the street that I bet just dump straight into the river. The people stink, too. Don't they ever shower?"

"They explained that to us, Sarge. Most of them don't have any hot water. And soap is rationed to two cakes a month per family." He elbowed the sergeant. "Bet you need that much soap every time you shower to smell good."

"Ha ha ha. You're a laugh riot, Joe," grumbled the sergeant. "Listen, kid," he said to Henry, "just watch you don't get soaked. All of Paris is a clip joint as far as I'm concerned. They charge ninety francs for one shot of watered-down cognac. I went to the Folies Bergère and the usher girl demanded a tip for showing me to my seat. What a racket!"

"But they don't pay them anything," the private interrupted again. "It's like our tipping taxi drivers or redcaps. It's how they make a living." The private turned to Henry. "It's worth a tip just to meet them, sir. They are some of the prettiest gals I've ever seen. And real nice if you talk to them. Of course, they don't hold a candle to my Millie, but it's fun to look." He grinned.

"Well, they won't look back," grumbled the sergeant. "The French don't like us, Joe. I'm telling you. They never thank us for anything. Since October our engineer corps has removed thirty demolished bridges and built two new ones across the Seine. But all the French do is complain that we have too good of a time when we're on leave. Complain, complain, complain."

The private looked at Henry and rolled his eyes as if to say, *Look who's talking*. "Here's where you start, sir. Go to Rainbow Corner, run by the Red Cross. They'll help you find rooms rented out by the French. But don't worry. If you get in a pinch, there are plenty of us around to help you out. Besides us with the quartermaster unit, thousands of GIs come in on leave every week."

"He don't need the Rainbow Corner," said the sergeant, turning to eye Henry for the first time. "Somehow he rates the Hotel Scribe. That's where we're supposed to direct him."

Surprised, the private shifted his weight and his attitude

the way enlisted gunners on the aircrew would change when an officer came in the room. Clearly he was no longer as comfortable with Henry.

"I didn't arrange for any room yet," said Henry.

"No, sir," the sergeant answered. "But it's been put in for you. By the same brass that gave you that stash."

He referred to the Red Cross relief box Henry was holding in his lap. It had appeared in the truck, labeled for him. It was crammed full of supplies: K-ration biscuits, Klim powdered milk, Kraft cheese, Sun-Maid raisins, Jack Frost sugar, Hershey bars, instant coffee, and yes, Spam. Henry'd been grateful for the food, figuring that was a fair handout to compensate for the things the police had taken from him. But he was beginning to feel a little funny at the mention of the hotel. "What's the big deal about the Hotel Scribe?"

"It's pretty swank, sir. It's where all the newspaper guys are housed. Used to be the hotel for the Nazi propaganda unit, so it stayed pretty well outfitted during the war. The Army guys brief you daily and keep a good eye on you, sir."

So that's why the private suddenly seemed uneasy around him. They thought Henry was press. All the fliers had been leery of reporters when they met them on the base. They seemed nice enough, but if a flier was quoted in a real honest moment, he could get into a barrage of flak with his superiors.

"I'm not a newsman."

They both looked at him with that "Sure, right" expression Henry knew so well from his time with the guys in his base Nissen hut. "Then why the red carpet?" the sergeant asked.

Henry didn't know. But he was beginning to worry about Thurman's long-term expectations of him. If Clayton had taught Henry one thing, it was to stand on his own two feet. Maybe Clayton's reasons for that had been to avoid obligations he didn't like the smell of.

About the time they started driving alongside the Seine River and seeing rows of tall, meticulously kept town houses, they heard church bells. Cannon fire. The rushing sweep of planes.

"What's going on?" the private asked.

Henry held on to the rim of the window and pushed himself out to look at the belly of low-flying planes. They were American B-17s. "They're fortresses!" he called back into the truck cab. Was the city under attack? That wouldn't make any sense given their formation, and how low they were flying. If the Germans had launched some sort of counterattack, the Allies would be answering with fighters, not bombers.

Suddenly there was a racket of horn blowing—cars, trucks, unseen but heard for miles. And a kind of roar rose from deep inside the city, as if thousands of people were crying out. Unnerved, Henry poked his head back into the truck. "What do you think it is?"

For the first time, the sergeant cracked a grin that sweetened his sour face. He slammed on the brakes and the convoy following stopped short, in a domino of screeches. Cheering erupted from the back of the line and rolled up along the trucks to them, as the sergeant held up his fingers in a V, like Churchill.

Could it be?

"We've won!" the sergeant cried. "We've won, Joe. I heard a rumor about it this morning. Hitler killed himself and the Nazis have finally surrendered."

"We've won? It's over?" the private repeated in awed tones. Then the two of them screamed it out together over and over in shouts of delight and relief: "We've won! We've won!" They jumped out of the cab to join a dozen drivers skipping, embracing, knocking one another over, like a mass of puppies playing.

Everywhere around them doors flung open and French children, women, men spilled out, crying, *"Victoire! Victoire!"*

Somehow, carried by a mass of dancing, rejoicing people, Henry ended up on the Champs-Élysées, the main boulevard of Paris. From the Arc de Triomphe to the huge palace of the Louvre, the street was jammed full of jeeps and taxis and bodies. Every U.S. Army vehicle was covered with girls waving handkerchiefs, waving flags, blowing kisses, singing snatches of American songs they'd learned from the radio: *"Yez, zir, zat's my bébé."* Thousands marched up and down, crying and laughing, chanting, *"Vive la France! Vive la France!"* White and pink petals from the blossoming chestnut trees fell like confetti on them. American planes roared overhead.

Watching the formations, Henry got drenched when sculpture fountains that had been dry and silent during the war were turned on suddenly in coughing spews of water. Parisians clapped and splashed the water at one another, the cascading fountains adding to the city's raucous partying. French troops on horseback and in Napoleonic dress uniforms tried to parade, but the crowds swallowed them and hoisted girls up onto the horses. Wrapping their arms around the soldiers, they squealed as the horsehair plumes from the men's shining helmets fell into their faces.

Because of his conversation with Thurman, Henry wondered at the sight of Soviet soldiers in fancy high collars, red stars, and shoulder-board epaulets walking arm-in-arm with American GIs—no political distrust between them, just rejoicing in peace. But Henry couldn't contemplate that long as a child grabbed his hand and dragged him into a conga line. The elderly, the elegant, the ragged stretched for yards, connected hands to hips, sashaying in time like a giant centipede of joy.

At twilight red, white, and blue floodlights lit up the city's most famous monuments—the Arc de Triomphe, the Place de la Concorde, and the Opera. There was a momentary hush as the lights switched on. Then the masses began to sing a Resistance song that filled Henry with a bittersweet pride of mourning and celebration:

When they poured across the border,
I was cautioned to surrender.
This I could not do.
I took my gun and vanished.
I have changed my name so often;
I've lost my wife and children.
But I have many friends
And some of them are with me.

An old woman gave us shelter,
Kept us hidden in the garret.
Then the soldiers came.
She died without a whisper.
There were three of us this morning,
I'm the only one this evening.
But I must go on
The frontiers are my prison.

Oh, the wind, the wind is blowing,
Through the graves the wind is blowing.
Freedom soon will come
Then we'll come from the shadows.

So many had died for this moment—May 8, 1945, Victory in Europe, VE Day the crowds called it. Henry promised himself to mark the date in the years ahead by remembering Madame, Dan, Billy, and his teenage guide. They would be his partners in any dance of celebration. Their memory followed him through that night of rejoicing.

At midnight, the Parisian fire brigade blew trumpets to end the official partying. Shouldering his bag, Henry set off to find the Hotel Scribe, following directions scribbled down by the convoy's sergeant.

Tomorrow his hunt for Pierre would begin again. Tomorrow, perhaps he'd find him. Then the war for Henry would finally be over.

CHAPTER TWENTY

Around two A.M., Henry stumbled through the revolving door of the Hotel Scribe. He'd been lost for a good hour. The hotel was near the landmark Opera House, which was straight up the Avenue de l'Opéra from the Louvre. But the neighborhood was dark and confusing. For years the city had been operating in blackout mode against potential Allied or Nazi raids and electricity had yet to be really restored. The end of the war had brought a sudden, strange juxtaposition of lighting. The streets were illuminated by moonlight, candles from inside buildings, and ricochets of white beams from the newly lit floodlights on the Opera House about a half mile up the boulevard.

Once he found his way to the avenue, Henry felt like a moth drawn to a porch light. He'd never, ever, in his entire life seen anything as fancy as the enormous Opera House. The building had to be a couple of acres big. The walls were covered with statues of dancers, musicians, cupids, and Grecian women, all surrounded with stone wreaths or framed in arches. As he walked along its edge to take a left onto the rue Scribe, he gaped at two huge, winged golden statues perched on the roof's corners that seemed big enough to carry the building off. He nearly ran into a street lamp, he was staring so.

He felt even more the country bumpkin inside the hotel. Although it smelled of tobacco and flat champagne, leftovers of the day's excitement, the lobby was intimidatingly elegant. Painted frescoes covered the walls; columns held up the vaulted ceiling, and from it swung cut-glass chandeliers the size of hay bales. He was almost relieved that no one was behind the wood-paneled desk. He sat down in a soft armchair in the corner, figuring he'd wait for a clerk to show up. He leaned his head up against the chair wing to keep watch. Within ten minutes he was asleep.

"Excusez-moi."

Sunlight and a musical voice woke Henry.

A young woman was talking with a desk clerk. *"Pourrais-je laisser un message pour Monsieur Hemingway?"*

The clerk told her there was no Hemingway staying at the hotel.

She frowned. *"Ernest Hemingway? Mais il m'a dit qu'il logeait ici."*

Ernest Hemingway? Staying here? Henry sat up. He knew that name from his crew navigator, Fred Bennett. Fred had made it through two years at Harvard before joining up. He was a literature major and was forever telling Henry about books he should read. A few nights before their plane was hit, Fred had had a few too many beers and ranted on and on about a Hemingway book called *For Whom the Bell Tolls*. Henry remembered the title because it sounded so ominous, almost as if Fred had had a premonition. Poor Fred. Henry flinched at the memory of his body in the nose of the plane. He would have been so excited to meet a real live author.

The desk clerk was trying to shoo off the girl. He clearly thought she was someone Hemingway would not want to be bothered by. She clutched a bundle of papers. She had met Hemingway at a bookstore. He had promised to look at her novel when she was done. Well, she said, she was done. And she wanted to find him. He had promised.

A tall, gaunt man entered the hotel as this was going on. He leaned up against the desk, waiting to collect his key and messages.

"*Sortez.*" The clerk waved his hand at the girl in final dismissal. Monsieur Hemingway would not be interested in the likes of her, he said.

"Oh, I think he would be," the gaunt man broke in. He had a thin, clipped moustache, and when he smiled it stretched itself and wiggled. His voice was clipped, too, British. In perfect French he told the girl that he knew Hemingway. The writer was lodging at the Ritz. He leaned close to her to say in a stage whisper that it had a better bar. The girl was out the door in a flash.

The clerk thanked the man. The things he had to deal with, he complained—lovesick girls, pushy journalists, rude Americans sleeping in the lobby. He glanced down his nose at Henry. Embarrassed, Henry stood. He hadn't meant to fall asleep. He'd admit he was scroungy-looking, but that was because he'd only been able to take one real bath, at Madame's house, since landing in France. He brushed himself off to approach the desk.

"Je suis une chambre pour louer," Henry tried asking for a room.

The clerk sniffed and stared at him scornfully. Henry repeated himself. The clerk smirked.

With a sympathetic smile, the Brit put his hand on Henry's shoulder. "You are not a room for hire. What you wish to say, I assume, is that you have a room and you want your key. That is: *J'ai une chambre ici et je voudrais ma clé."*

Henry turned sunburn red and repeated the Brit's wording.

Only then did the clerk switch to English. "I have no rooms available."

Henry started to step away, too embarrassed by his mistakes and the clerk's hostility to argue.

"Tell him your name, lad. It might be under that."

Henry did so. With irritated drama, the clerk searched through cards. He paused over one and glanced up at Henry and then at the paper again. "Pardon, *monsieur*. You should have said you were with the OSS. We have rooms for them on the third floor." He reached for a key.

"I'm not OSS," Henry said.

The clerk shoved the key at Henry and was done with him. He handed the Brit a few messages. "Dining room open?" the man asked. The clerk nodded and the man headed for the wide marble steps leading downstairs. "Better work on that French, my friend, if you're going to be intelligence," he said as he disappeared.

"But I'm not OSS," Henry muttered as he closed himself into the birdcage elevator and pushed the number three. After a few moments of waiting, he realized there was no electricity. The clerk sniggered as Henry headed for the staircase.

Up on the third floor, Henry stood listening to a dozen typewriters clacking and newsmen shouting questions to one another about de Gaulle; the size of the previous day's crowd; Eisenhower's whereabouts; how the Americans, Brits, and Soviets would divvy up Germany among themselves for occupation; and whether France would be given a zone as well. Voices came in English and a hodgepodge of languages Henry was unsure of—Italian, Swedish, Spanish maybe. He passed a door with the sign WIDEWING, USSTAF and another with GANGWAY, 9TH AIR FORCE PUBLIC RELATIONS. The doors were open and inside lieutenants were busily typing.

Henry passed more rooms, marked with signs like PRESS WIRELESS, until he came to the end of the hall. His room was long, a narrow closet really, but it had a nice single bed with crisp white linen and a washstand with towels. Henry wanted a real bath. He made his way back to the Air Force office to ask where the showers were.

"Down the hall, Mac, around the corner." A corporal pointed the way. "You're new, right?" He didn't really wait for an answer or introduction. "Better hoof it. The water's heated from seven to ten A.M. Most everyone's going to be heading that way soon after getting their stories filed."

The water was lukewarm, but Henry was very grateful to be clean, his hair blond again instead of a strange color of greasy. Shaved and dry, he figured he'd treat himself to something decent to eat and headed downstairs.

In the dining room, most of the men there had their heads on the tables, trying to recover from the night's celebrations. Only the Brit who'd helped Henry seemed wide awake. He'd finished eating and was pouring loose tobacco into paper to roll his own cigarette. He wore a blue flannel shirt and his leather jacket hung on the back of his chair—unusual workingman clothes in the collection of officer uniforms, tweed jackets, and silk ties around him.

Henry decided to thank him for the help with the desk clerk and his clumsy French. "Thanks for bailing me out, mister. I never seem to get my French quite right. Nearly got killed last year because of it." He put out his hand, "My name's Henry Forester."

The man licked the edge of his cigarette paper, rolled it tight, and stuck it into his mouth before taking Henry's hand. "Orwell, George. Have a seat."

"Oh no, sir, I don't want to interrupt."

Orwell extended his arms. "What's to interrupt? I'm the only sober man here and that's only barely."

Henry gratefully sat down and was amazed when the waiter offered him poached eggs and white toast with jam. He looked up at Orwell in surprise before digging into his food with a vengeance.

"Enjoy. Only in the Scribe will you find such fare. The Americans ship it in. Sometimes there is a line of Parisians out back hoping for scraps, like something from the eighteenth century. Been a while since you've eaten?"

Self-consciously wiping his mouth with a big white napkin, Henry nodded.

"No offense, my boy, but you really don't fit the OSS.

You are going to stand out like a sore thumb. There are a number of British and American intelligence officers in this hotel. You're nothing like them. Maybe you're clerical support?" he asked hopefully.

"I'm *not* OSS, sir. I'm not anything at all."

"What are you doing here then?"

Henry hesitated.

"It's all right," Orwell said. "We can make it off the record. I'm in need of a good story right now. And I can tell you have one."

Henry assessed his face. There were dark circles under the man's deep-set eyes. His skin was stretched taut and pale over high cheekbones. He was probably around forty and looked sickly, sad. Something about his melancholy told Henry that he would understand.

So he told him. Told him about being shot down, being saved, and his search for Pierre. The man nodded and listened, pulling long inhalations of his cigarette. He was so attentive, Henry even admitted to his nightmares, and his hopes that Patsy would think he was ready to restart his life when he came home.

He finished by telling Orwell that he had wheedled himself out of arrest. The only part Henry omitted was exactly how he did that. He left out the Nazi nested in with the Americans. Instinctively Henry knew that keeping that information to himself was the only reason he was still in

France. Divulge it and he broke the unspoken pact with Thurman. And somehow, Henry sensed, Thurman would hear of it if he did. He was getting the distinct feeling of being shadowed by the man.

When he was done, he felt emptied.

Orwell coughed, a hacking rattle, and then tipped onto the back two legs of his chair, putting his hands behind his head. "When was the last time you flew over Germany?"

"March last year."

"Then you haven't seen the absolute devastation dropped out of the sky by your bombers. I've just come back from Nuremberg and Stuttgart, covering Allied movements for the *Observer*. German cities are ruins. Every bridge, every train, every viaduct in the three hundred miles between the Marne and Rhine rivers was blown up. Europe will suffer a long poverty before we can build things back to the standard of living of the Depression, let alone anything better."

He rocked forward and leaned toward Henry. "If you find this boy, and his mother is dead as you fear, you should take him home to America. He'll end up in an orphanage here. He'll be marginalized, a third-class citizen."

Take Pierre home? Henry hadn't thought of that before. "Why do you think he'd be . . . did you say 'marginalized,' sir?"

"I fear France will not break apart its class structure

any time soon, no matter what its socialist intellectuals and Resistance fighters say. De Gaulle's nationalism feels very old school, very *bourgeois*, the French would call it. I suspect, sadly, that the emphasis will be on getting France back to the way it was—the cabarets, the fashion makers, the superb wine—not making life better for orphans or ordinary people. But I hope I am wrong."

He thought a moment and added, "Be careful around the Scribe, Henry. The OSS seems interested in you. You must know something or they think you'll lead them to people they want to watch. When the government wants something, it has a way of dogging you. Before you know it, someone may convince you to do something without your even realizing you're doing it."

Orwell reached around to pull his coat from the back of his chair. As he did, Henry caught a glimpse of a pistol stuffed inside the breast pocket.

"Whoa," Henry murmured, and pushed back from the table.

For a moment Orwell looked puzzled. "Ah, yes. I carry this for protection. Ever since I wrote about the betrayal of the workers' revolution in Spain by the Communist party and the Soviet secret police, I have been afraid of a Stalin-ordered hit. The Soviets are feeling very bold right now. All sorts of retributions are happening in dark streets. And I'm about to publish something that Stalin is sure to hate."

He stood up and shook Henry's hand good-bye. "I'm leaving for Austria. Remember what I've told you about the OSS. I know. I did a stint with the BBC in its India section, wanting to help the war effort. But I was sickened by writing propaganda. It's twisting reality, presenting things to promote the government's agenda, manipulating words to indoctrinate—to make us sheep."

Orwell contemplated Henry for a moment. "Just like farm animals," he muttered more to himself than to Henry. Henry tried not to squirm under the gaze.

"You strike me as being an idealist, like me," Orwell continued. "Face it—your time of influence here is over, lad. That's true of all good soldiers. The aftermath of war is a messy, brutal elbowing among political ideologies, as different groups that survived the war battle each other for power. They will smile at one another's faces while plotting coups and spying on each other."

"Sir? What are you talking about?" Henry asked. "Peace has been declared."

"Peace? Peace is not that easy, that finite, my boy. War ends; then it takes a long time to negotiate a real truce. Many times that peace is troubled and contains the embers for the next war, smoldering, just in need of a spark. Take France. There is already friction between de Gaulle and the communist-dominated Resistance, mainly because de Gaulle has been lenient with collaborators. He's making all sorts of compromises to push France forward. Meanwhile, the Soviets and the Americans circle, both hoping to influence France to adopt their way of doing things, both snooping and trying to undermine each other. Stalin seems bent on taking over as much of Europe as possible now that Hitler is out of the way. Stalin is as vicious as Hitler in how he crushes people he feels are inferior or who stand up to him. The U.S. will use any means to stop him. There's sure to be a rather nasty standoff, perhaps right here in France, beginning with covert politics."

Henry thought of the angry disappointment of the Marseille restaurant owner, the Vercors doctor's suspicions of de Gaulle, and Thurman's attempt to coerce Henry to name communist *maquis* he'd met so that the OSS could spy on them.

Orwell put his hand on Henry's shoulder once more. "Right and wrong will no longer be clear, not like the target of your bomb runs were. You'll have trouble getting your bearings. If I were you, Henry, I'd go home as soon as possible. Good luck."

Henry watched Orwell leave. If only the man knew how much Henry had already compromised himself to be in Paris. Go home as soon as possible? For sure—but not until he found Pierre.

Chapter Twenty-one

Outside, Henry headed for Gare de l'Est, the train station of the East. He followed the map of Paris that a GI handed him. With a girl on each arm, still celebrating victory, the soldier joked that he had his own personal guides. "They're going to show me the Eiffel Tower and then my seventy-two hours of freedom are over. It's back on a train to my outfit near Stuttgart." He pointed up the boulevard as the threesome strolled away. "The Gare de l'Est is that way."

Henry was glad to have the map to reassure him that he was going the right way since the wide avenue kept changing names. The buildings all looked the same, too—long, connecting facades of smooth mortar running flat to the street, five to seven stories high. Their beauty and individuality came in small touches of decoration, in high archways carved with lions' heads or fleurs-de-lis. Windows were almost as tall and wide as double doors, and many were whiskered with beautiful wrought iron balconies, the black metal twisted into curling vines and flowers. The buildings were gray from decades of soot belched out of charcoal fires, giving a pen-and-ink-sketch look to the streets. Even so, on this bright sunny morning, they were the prettiest he'd ever seen.

Many of the first floors housed bookstores, clothing shops, or grocers. Looking in, Henry could tell the owners had put most of their wares in the display window. Shelves inside were empty, the rooms dark. As he walked, the city awoke. More people began to enter the street. No cars appeared, but bicycles crowded the road. Small cabs, pulled by men on bicycles, lumbered by. Gangs of girls with billowing skirts and long legs zipped past them. Henry was nearly run down by a boy pushing a wheelbarrow as fast as he could so that the huge block of ice inside wouldn't melt before he got it home.

Along came an elderly man in a boater hat and a slightly frayed but smart suit and ascot. He leaned on a gold-capped walking cane. In the other hand he balanced a fishing pole and a small basket. He was obviously heading for the Seine. A GI threw a cigarette butt into the gutter near him. Stiffly, the old man leaned over for it. He stuck it into a long cigarette holder, the kind Henry had seen in Fred Astaire and Ginger Rogers movies depicting the Jazz Age.

Henry realized the holder would allow the man to drain the cigarette to its last drop of nicotine. He wished he had those Camel cigarettes now. He'd gladly give the old gentleman a pack to restore his dignity.

Uncomfortable, Henry hurried on, hoping that now the war against Hitler was over, things could get back to normal quickly. Although given Orwell's description of the devastation across Europe, it could take years just to clear away the rubble.

At the train station, hundreds of grim people waited in front of the platforms. An anxious murmuring, amplified by the white marble floors, lifted as a hum toward the lofty glass ceilings. *How much longer till the train pulls in? Do you think he'll be on this one? They say three thousand will come through today. Have you heard how thin they are, covered with sores and lice? Awful.* Quelle horreur!

A woman cried out and dropped a newspaper. After her friends guided her to a bench, Henry picked it up. He gagged. There was a photograph from a concentration camp named Bergen-Belsen—a long pit with rows of corpses in it, naked, mangled, the bodies so emaciated they were barely identifiable as human. Next to it was an article saying prisoners were being shot right before the Allies liberated camps. Bodies were still warm when the soldiers entered. They had been that close to freedom when killed.

"Ils arrivent!" someone cried. The "absents" were pulling into the station.

The crowd pushed forward. Those in front began to sing in greeting, and the lyrics rippled back to where Henry stood, those around him picking up the verse: *"C'est la route qui va, qui va, qui va."* Then, just as suddenly, silence rolled back, the singing abruptly stopping. The crowd parted and two soldiers come through carrying a man—if you could call the poor soul that. He looked more like a stick-figure hangman drawing than a real body. His bone-thin arms were around their necks and he sat in a cradle the soldiers easily made with their own strong, thick forearms. Wearing striped pajamas, he grimaced with pain. Or was that his smile?

More were carried out. Then those who could walk began to stagger through.

Get back, the soldiers shouted. The absents had not yet gone through quarantine and could carry typhus.

But when people recognized a ghostly figure, they burst through the crowd, with both cries of joy and horror, gathering their loved one up in kiss-filled embraces. Others rushed forward and then stood woodenly, shocked, bewildered, repulsed. The deportees held out what little bundle they might clutch and dutifully waited to be told what to do.

Most of the returned trudged on, following the back of the person in front to the doors that opened onto the wide boulevard de Strasbourg. There U.S. Army trucks driven by Free French soldiers waited to transport them to the repatriation center at Hotel Lutetia. Only a few blinked in the warm sunbeams sifting through the leaded glass ceiling of the train station and looked up to the vast half-moon window that opened the wall to a brilliant blue sky and sun-haloed clouds. Golden light lit up the sunrise design and its latticework rays that stretched out wide, ending in a lacy outline of smaller starbursts.

One woman stopped when she saw it. Those behind her simply walked around, like water rushing past a stone in a creek. She stayed rooted, her eyes lifted. *"Mon Dieu,"* she murmured, tears streaming down her face. *"C'est le ciel de Paris."* The Paris sky, just as she remembered it. *Exactement.* The Nazis could not change that.

Only later, when hearing how so many had left Paris from that very station, crammed into cattle cars heading to Germany, to be herded off the trains into warehouses and gassed, could Henry completely understand the symbolism of her return and her awe. At that moment, he simply caught his breath, recognizing another human being slipping the surly bonds of earth, climbing sunward, and finding redemption in the sky. He was witnessing a rebirth. He would never forget the sight of it.

Nor would he forget that after that woman walked on—smiling, transformed, beautiful again—and the wave of deportees had swept by, in its wake were left two little girls. Just as Madame had described, they held up signs carefully penned with their full names, their last names large. They wore embroidered sweaters, carefully pressed pleated skirts, and huge butterfly bows pulling back their shining hair, their faces as hopeful as those Sunday-best clothes.

When the last deportee walked out the door, and no parent had come, and no news of them either, the children wilted. Silently, the oldest took her sister's hand. Heads down, they left the train station, their signs bumping along the pavement.

CHAPTER TWENTY-TWO

Henry followed them, remembering that Madame Gaulloise said children looked for their parents at the train station or the Hotel Lutetia. He figured they would go there next.

The little girls went down the Boulevard de Strasbourg, past a huge market and hordes of people haggling over crates of fruits and vegetables, to the Seine. They crossed over it and an island with what must have been Notre Dame, given the long, carved stone braces that jutted out from the cathedral—Miss Dixon had called them flying buttresses. The girls kept walking. Henry kept shadowing them.

For an hour they walked—no childhood skipping or dallying, no pausing by the one shop that had sweets in its window or to watch the hobo street performer with a small scraggly dog sitting on his head. They didn't slow until they turned from the Boulevard Saint Germain onto the rue du Four. Many blocks down, another crowd gathered. Unlike the one at Gare de l'Est, this one was loud.

Frustrated shouts echoed up the street. People were crammed against a barricade and shaking their fists at police who pushed them back with sticks. Even more people jostled in front of billboards nailed to poles and littered with papers on both sides. The people in back barked at those ahead for standing too long, for blocking the view. Those closest to the boards snarled at them for pushing from behind.

What does that one say? I can't read it. There were cries of anguish, people collapsing onto curbs to cry. Or sparks of hope—*Look, look there! Do you see? A month ago!*

What in the world were they looking at? Gingerly, Henry stepped into the rumbling crowd.

Photos. Hand-scrawled notes:

If you know of Etienne Cain, please contact Rebecca Cain, 9, rue Gabrielle.

Tell the family of Marcel Challe that their son was alive as of April 15.

Or on some of the photos, messages like this one beside a formal portrait of a beautiful young woman at a piano: *I am very sorry. Your daughter died October 1944. Before that she would sing 'Che tua madre' from* Madama

Butterfly *to us. She brought beauty to Ravensbruck.*

Henry backed away, knowing this was no place for an idle spectator. It was a horrible way to learn the fate of a loved one. Or to learn nothing at all.

He searched for the girls. Relieved, he spotted them crossing the street to a park, where an elderly lady sat. They helped her stand and supported her arms as they walked away. Well, at least someone was watching over them, Henry mused, although it looked like the children were taking care of the lady more than the other way around.

Henry jogged across and took the bench. He tried to regather himself. No one stateside would believe all this, he thought.

A long line of exhausted, frail deportees waiting to be processed inched its way along the wall toward the entrance of the Hotel Lutetia. Official-looking women in tightly buttoned navy blue uniforms marched up and down, scribbling on clipboards, asking questions. Bystanders shouted their own: *Do you have any news of* ——? Dozens of names were called at the same time, peppering the deportees like scattershot from shotguns. They looked dazed. Only a few managed replies. The French soldiers guarding them did nothing to stop the incessant, frantic interrogation. *Do you know of* ——? *Have you seen* ——? Only when one woman doubled over as if kicked in the stomach and started screaming at a deportee that she was a liar—her sister could not be dead—*liar, liar, liar*—did the soldiers pull someone away from the line.

Another truck convoy arrived, depositing more deportees. Unsteady, those men shuffled into the already long line.

Henry despaired. Where in the world among all these people, in this huge city, did he think he'd find one small, lost, unhappy boy?

Henry watched all afternoon, approaching any children he saw, listening, searching their faces for any familiar features. He realized how much a nine-year-old boy could grow in a year, how much starvation could alter a person's face. Would he recognize Pierre?

At twilight, following playground sounds of laughter and jeering, Henry entered the park behind him. It was a pretty little square of pine and gum trees, pebble walkways, and flower beds, an oasis from the noise and angst of the street outside. At its entrance was a marble statue of three figures: a small boy climbing stairs to two women in long coats and muffs, one elderly, one young. The women's carved faces carried concern for the stone boy, who held his hat in his hand. The older lady was leaning down to rest her hand on the child's shoulder. The younger one

looked to be pulling money from her purse. At the base of
the stairs was a fourth stone figure, a new mother holding an infant, carefully shielding the baby with her chiseled cloak. The work was marked: MADAME BOUCICANT
1816–1887 and MADAME DE HIRSCH 1833–1899. Henry felt his
throat tighten at its symbol of need, replicated so clearly
in real-life souls across the street.

The laughter came from behind the statue's stairs.
Henry had already figured out that getting too close to the
children hanging around the hotel caused them to skitter
away. Henry tiptoed up the stairs and sat next to the stone
women, shielded from the children's view.

"Ton tour."

Henry peeped over and saw a game of what looked like
jacks. Patsy had played it constantly when they were kids.
But instead of a tiny rubber ball and little metal stars, these
boys and girls were hurling up a knobby bone painted red,
and scrambling to pick up a scattering of smaller bones
before it hit the ground again. Two boys were facing off.
They both made it through picking up pairs and triples.
But one of them failed to grab four before the red bone
came back down.

"Merde!" The loser handed over a stick of gum.

Henry's mouth dropped open at the sight of little kids
gambling.

The winner tried a new hustle. He presented a lumpy

leather sack and poured out a huge cache of marbles. He grinned, cocky. When no one would take him on, he ridiculed the group as cowards. *"Quels trouillards!"*

The boy sweetened his lure with *two* sticks of gum as his bet and offered to loan a special shooter he'd won the day before to whomever had the guts to play him. *"Regardez."* He held up a large marble, saying that it'd once belonged to an American and that the boy who lost it claimed it was good luck. He laughed with a grown man's sarcasm. *"Bonne chance pour moi!"*

It sure would help the player using it, thought Henry. It was a huge end-of-day "cloud," with red and gold swirls, a one-of-a-kind marble that glassblowers made from the day's leftover glass scraps. Just like the marble he'd won off Clayton and carried on bombing missions for good luck, the one he'd given Pierre.

Wait a minute. Henry's breath snagged. *Good luck. Red and gold swirls.* Henry couldn't keep himself from leaning over the edge to get a closer look.

As soon as his head appeared above them, the children shrieked and scattered. The boy scrambled to shove his marbles back into his bag before darting away. But Henry was too quick for him. He pole-vaulted over the back of the statue and grabbed the hustler by his wrist. The boy still clutched the marble.

Henry snatched it and turned it over and over, looking

for a tiny flaw, a little chip in one of the golden whirls.
There it was. This *was* his marble. He was certain of it.
But why wasn't it with Pierre? "Where did you get this?"
Henry nearly shouted the question.

The boy looked up at him with terrified eyes.

"Où est-ce que tu trouves ça?" Henry repeated in French.
"Please. I am looking for the boy this belonged to."

The boy shook his head, still frightened, clearly thinking Henry meant to hurt him. Henry was ashamed to be
terrorizing a child. He felt like Clayton. But Henry knew
that the instant he let go the hustler would bolt.

"Pierre. *Il s'appelle Pierre.* Do you know him?" Henry
was vaguely aware of the other children peeping out from
behind bushes and trees. "I won't hurt you. I promise. *Je
te promets.*"

"He does not believe you."

Henry turned around to see a short, middle-aged
woman in a white smock and scarf. As he looked, the boy
hauled off and punched him, right on his sore rib. Henry
gasped. His grip loosened. The boy wrenched free.

Henry lurched for him, just missing, and belly-flopped
on the pebbles.

The boy stumbled and righted himself and was about
to escape.

"Arrête, mon petit," the woman spoke gently and stepped
in his path. The boy froze. She held her hand up to stop

Henry from moving and spooking the child. "What is it you want from the boy?" she asked him. "Tell me and I will explain to him."

"I am looking for a boy named Pierre who saved my life. I am an American pilot. Pierre hid me and connected me with the *maquis*. His mother was taken to Ravensbruck. He comes from the Vercors. The rest of his family is dead. I am afraid she might be as well. I gave him this marble." He held it up. "That boy must know where Pierre is since he had the marble."

"The Vercors," the woman murmured. "God help him." She turned to the boy and explained in French. Did he know where Pierre was?

Henry's heart sank when the boy answered no. But he did add that Pierre had been hanging around, waiting for "an absent" to return.

Bingo. Madame Gaulloise had been right!

"*Merci, chéri.*" The woman pulled half a roll from her apron pocket and gave it to the boy, who grabbed it. He ran off, cramming huge bites into his mouth, trailed by the other children, like gulls chasing a bird that had caught a fish along the James River back home. The sight sickened Henry. Pierre was probably that hungry, too.

Henry pushed himself to his feet and carefully buttoned the marble in his pocket. "Thank you, *madame.*"

She looked him over, finally smiling slightly. "You will

not find your Pierre by threatening other children."

Henry flinched at the word *threatening*. "I didn't mean to scare him," he explained, feeling like he'd been caught in a schoolyard fight.

"These children are damaged," the woman continued quietly as if explaining something quite obvious to the class dunce. "They are afraid. Many live on the streets as they watch and pray for parents to return. They are terrified of being caught and taken to an orphanage or something worse. They will not trust anything you say. Too many of their loved ones have disappeared, right after someone like you asked questions."

Henry nodded. He could see it. But what should he do, then—wait outside the hotel and just hope he could collar Pierre and hang on to him until he could talk the boy into trusting him again? If the past months had affected Pierre in the same way they had this gang, Henry knew that plan had a snowball's chance in Hades.

"Can you help me, *madame*?" It was obvious from her hospital smock and scarf that she was with the Lutetia's deportation center. "Please? I'm a good worker. I could do whatever you need at the hotel until we find him or his mother."

The woman thought a moment, then motioned for Henry to follow her to the long row of boards. They had been pushed up under the hotel's awnings to protect them during the night. Only a few people remained reading the notices. She pulled a small pad of paper from her pocket. "What is the boy's full name?"

"Pierre Dubois."

"The mother's?"

"I don't know, *madame*." Again, Henry kicked himself for not asking the priest when he had the chance.

"Hmmmm. That will make it harder." She thought a bit before writing.

The setting sun cast a red glow on the hundreds of faces pinned there. Among them, at a child's eye level, she tacked her square note: *Pierre Dubois, please come inside and ask for Sabine Zlatin.*

"We shall see if this works. It may frighten him off at first. So you must be patient. What is your name?"

"Henry Forester, *madame*."

"Come back tomorrow, Monsieur Forester. We can use you."

"Yes, ma'am!" Hope raced through him. "What time?"

"Before the first train of deportees arrives. At six thirty. Now that victory is declared, the Allies are free to help move the absents. The Americans have been flying in thousands from Germany each day. They tell us to expect eight thousand tomorrow."

CHAPTER TWENTY-THREE

The next morning, Madame Zlatin put Henry to work disinfecting the deportees' tattered clothes. She gave him a surgical mask and a hand-pumped spray can full of DDT. "Work quickly," she told him. "The clothes are covered with lice that carry typhus. The disease killed thousands at the camps."

Henry pumped the plunger of that can until he thought his arm would fall off. He refilled it a dozen times, wreathing himself in clouds of dank, chemical smells. And still there were clothes tossed out across tables needing to be deloused. Every time he finished, nurses came carrying more bundles. Henry began to feel like Sisyphus in the Camus book that Madame Gaulloise had given him. Sisyphus, according to mythology, was condemned by the Greek gods to spend eternity pushing a boulder up a mountain only to have it roll back down again. Henry found the hopelessness of Sisyphus's labor, his inability to change his fate, incredibly annoying. He couldn't figure why it had been so important to Madame Gaulloise that he read it.

At noon, his head banging from the DDT fumes, Henry begged for a break.

The nurses nodded but asked him to hurry. As soon as the deportees had showered, they needed to put their clothes back on. Stripped of their possessions over and over again by the Nazis, these clothes were all the deportees had left. If there were new clothes to be found, the government promised to give them first to the million returning French POW soldiers.

Outside, Henry found the same chaos as before. He waded through the crowd to the board. The note for Pierre was still there. He scanned the street. Nothing.

He re-entered the hotel through the front door, under a carving of a great ship framed with smiling cherubs holding huge bunches of grapes, and squeezed past families begging to speak to officials. He found Madame Zlatin in the hotel's massive kitchens. She was explaining how much of the stew and pureed potatoes each deportee should receive. The sicker ones, those who weighed forty-eight kilograms or less, about a hundred pounds, could only eat broth, she said.

Henry marveled at how many pots were full and boiling. "Wow, *madame*, where did you come up with all this?"

"The deportees are given the highest priority for food." With a wry smile she added, "Much of this comes courtesy of the Reich. During the occupation, Hitler's Abwehr, his counterintelligence, was housed here. His officers demanded the same grandeur the hotel had offered guests before the war—caviar, champagne, cabaret performances. But when the battle for Paris began, the Nazis left the cold rooms stocked to the rafters with lamb and pork, cheeses and wines." She shrugged. "So we make good use of it."

Henry asked if she had heard anything about Pierre.

"No, *monsieur*. Patience."

"Patience-smatience," Henry muttered to himself as he went back to work.

When twilight fell, Henry fled the Lutetia. He'd had enough of its sad sights for the day. He was relieved that he'd had no flashbacks sparked by what he was witnessing. Lilly's voice came to him. *Sometimes you get back on your feet better when you're helping someone else stand in the process.* Maybe so. Seeing other people fight to survive, to walk away from the agonies they'd endured, was definitely prodding him to do likewise. Realizing that he was not the only one confronting personal demons also helped Henry to feel a little less like a freak. Plus, having a purpose—finding Pierre—gave him direction. He was beginning to feel like an effective human being again. But he realized his redemption hinged completely on finding Pierre.

Henry went to the notice boards. The note to Pierre was still pinned in the same spot. Henry searched the park. It was empty, the little gang gone, perhaps hiding from him. The only people there were a few deportees who had slipped out of the hotel. They sat on the park benches, gazing up at the flowering trees, smiling, free. Henry knew they were supposed to stay inside as the staff nursed them back to health. But he sure wasn't going to tell on them.

The next day passed in the same manner. And the next three. Henry must have asked Madame Zlatin a dozen times a day if she'd heard anything. "No, *monsieur*, nothing yet," she always answered gently. Finally, she told Henry to trust her. "There are many of us watching for Pierre and his mother. We will not forget. The absents do not forget either. They read our notes, looking to help us know the fate of those who are lost. Even amid the sorrows of thousands, we all know that we must restore the world one child at a time."

She glided away. "Now that is one kind lady," Henry murmured. "Just like Ma." The nurse folding towels near him looked up, thinking he was talking to her.

"*Elle est gentille.*" He repeated that Madame was kind.

"*Oui,*" the nurse agreed, "*la Dame d'Izieu est très gentille.*"

"I meant Madame Zlatin."

Another nurse explained. "We call her the Lady of Izieu because of the children."

"Children?"

"She hid forty-four Jewish children in the countryside near Izieu. One of her neighbors reported her to the Gestapo. They captured the children and sent them to Auschwitz. All of them were gassed to death. Madame escaped the raid because she was away trying to find other hiding places for them. Her husband was taken. His fate is unknown. She has put his picture on the wall with the others. She waits to learn."

Henry hung his head. *Forty-four children. Sweet Jesus.* Every story he heard put him in his place. He could find the patience to wait for Pierre to appear. At least he knew Pierre was alive.

Walking to the Hotel Scribe that evening, Henry purposefully turned up streets where he heard happy conversation. As he wandered, Henry felt compelled to reach out and touch the artistic decorations the French had chiseled into the stone of their buildings—tangible reminders that humans could produce beauty as well as devastation. He was particularly struck by a pair of marble doves roosting in the stone frame of a window that was pockmarked with bullet holes fanning out in a spiderweb of cracks—scars from the street fighting to liberate Paris.

He crossed the Boulevard Saint Germain to a cobblestone square with a medieval church in its center. The square was rimmed in cafés. One in particular was packed with people and raucous with arguments, jokes, singing, and glass-clinking toasts. Its tables spilled out under a dark green awning marked CAFÉ DES DEUX MAGOTS. Henry scratched his head—did that mean "the two maggots?" Well, he thought, he'd eaten snails with the *maquis,* and they'd been surprisingly tasty.

Henry thought about going in, but a group of women, enthusiastically shouting responses to a speaker deep in their circle, caught his attention. All Henry could see was a fist raised in the air above the other women's heads and a female voice calling, *"Maintenant nous pouvons voter!"* Now we women can vote!

"Bravo! Vive la France!"

"Nous-laisserons nous jamais réduire au silence de nouveau?" Will we allow ourselves to be silenced?

"Non!"

"Êtes-vous prêtes à toutes travailler ensemble?" Are you all ready to work together?

"Oui!"

The female voice went on to say that their work with the Resistance had shown women to be equal to men.

Women deserved equal pay and female delegates in the new legislature. Vote for women candidates! she shouted.

Listening, Henry could just imagine the comments his high school buddies would make: "Now why would the gals want to worry their pretty little heads over men's business?" Unlike the French, American women had been voting for decades. But Henry knew of only one woman ever elected to Congress. It'd be pretty amazing if the French actually voted in a few.

Boy, Patsy would love this, thought Henry. She hated having to package her thoughts into the ladylike manners the state of Virginia demanded. She was always getting herself in trouble at school for speaking her mind and questioning teachers. Her heroine was the outspoken Eleanor Roosevelt, even though half the country made fun of FDR's first lady, claiming she was unattractive and bossy.

A one-sheet newspaper was passed through the crowd. Titled *Femmes Françaises,* the paper had recipes for rutabagas and patterns for making children's shoes. But it also called for women to demonstrate against black marketers and for fairer rationing.

As the crowd broke up, Henry saw the back of the speaker. She wore a man's leather jacket and an odd skirt shaped like a lampshade that was made of panels of different materials, even silk scarves. She'd obviously had to make do with what she could scrounge. She also had on roller skates. That was clever, too, thought Henry, if she needed to cover a lot of ground quick, although going over cobblestones in those would be pretty teeth-rattling.

Henry wondered whether Pierre was clad in such a mishmash as well. He sighed, no longer distracted, and turned toward the river.

Suddenly from behind him came a *whirrrrrrrrrrrr* of metal wheels clattering over the stones. Before he could move out of the way, a hand grabbed Henry's elbow. The out-of-control speed of the roller skates hurled both him and the skater to the ground. With a curse, Henry landed face-first. The hand jerked him back and rolled him over.

"Mon Dieu. C'est toi! Henri!"

A girl with amber cat-eyes smothered him with kisses.

His mind spinning from the whack to his head and the embrace, Henry pushed her away, completely befuddled.

"Ah, once, you did not mind my kisses, Henri. Do you not know me? It is Claudette."

Henry stared. "Claudette?"

"Oui, oui! I thought you were dead. When you lured away those soldiers so that I could escape the Nazis, I feared they would shoot you. I cannot believe you live!"

Chapter Twenty-four

Henry had forgotten how insistent, how fiery, Claudette was. But it came back quickly as she pulled on his arm and demanded that he meet her friends. "I told them that an American saved me from capture. They must see that you survive. *C'est un miracle!*" She wasn't about to let go of his arm. And remembering how she'd flattened the Resistance fighter who had tried to run her out of the *maquis* camp, Henry wasn't about to argue.

He had not forgotten her beauty. She reminded him now of the Grecian-style marble women that held up the arches of the Opera House. With a long straight nose and high cheekbones, Claudette had a dramatic profile very like those of the chiseled statues. Her thick black eyebrows arched naturally, with none of that silly plucking the glamour girls did back home to create pencil-thin lines.

Her almond-shaped eyes were large and that unnerving yellow-green color. But it was her full lips that made her so exotic-looking. Patsy had lips like that, too, and seemed just as unaware as Claudette of how pretty they were.

Patsy. Henry felt a sudden pang of homesickness. And then a little twinge of guilt for appreciating Claudette's looks. Well, heck, he thought, Pats had turned him down, hadn't she? And here was this gorgeous French girl who was thrilled to see him. He pushed Patsy's memory aside and followed Claudette.

Claudette led them to a Metro stop, where she replaced her roller skates with wooden clogs she pulled from a straw bag. "No leather for slippers yet." She sighed. "These are so heavy. I prefer to skate, but I cannot walk stairs in them."

As she changed, a man crept from the dark stairwell, holding out a Hershey bar. *"Du chocolat américain,"* he hissed. *"Soixante francs."*

Henry stepped forward, instinctively shielding Claudette. But she brushed past him to hit the black marketer in the chest with her roller skates. *"Cochon!"*

The man howled in pain.

She swatted him again. "Black-marketers should get the death penalty! You sell things at such prices that we must bankrupt ourselves to eat. Because of you, children starve! Thief!"

Henry almost laughed. This was precisely what he recalled most about Claudette—a tiny spitfire taking on a squadron of enemies. But he also remembered that her self-righteous bravery threw her into danger constantly. Just as Claudette hauled off to hit the man again, he pulled a knife out of his pocket. The man jabbed at her, narrowly missing as Henry yanked her away and punched him in the face.

The man stumbled back spitting blood. All that boxing Henry's dad had forced him to do finally paid off! He'd have to remember to tell Clayton. Henry held up his fists—ready. "Come on!" But the man ran off instead, hurling insults at Claudette.

Claudette's eyes shone. She did love a fight, didn't she?

"I see you have regained your strength," she said. "No longer the half-starved boy I found stealing from my orchard." She took his hand again and led him down the dark stairs to the underground trains. They paid for second class, but she talked them into first, settling down on the upholstered benches with a sigh of contentment.

As the train rattled through the pitch-black tunnels, Claudette's lips brushed his again. "That is for saving my life for a second time," she whispered.

"Oh, that wasn't saving your life," Henry said of the man in the Metro. "You would have been all right."

"You are too modest, Henri." She kissed him again,

then pulled back and looked at him with puzzlement. "Why do you not return my kisses? Are you not happy to see me?"

"Lord, yes! I am so glad to see you, Claudette. You have no idea."

"Then why—?" She broke off abruptly, remembering. "Ah. The American girl, *oui*? Did you marry?"

Henry smiled ruefully. Ironically, the moment he and Claudette kissed in the Morvan a year ago was the moment when Henry realized clearly that he was, in fact, in love with Patsy. "No, we have not married." He paused, then added, "She turned me down."

"Oh, Henri," Claudette said sympathetically. "Then she is a fool." Claudette kissed him on the cheek.

This time Henry kissed her back.

They exited the Metro in the Montmartre district, climbing a hilltop of stairs to a huge, white, domed church that looked like something from India. "Basilique du Sacre Coeur," Claudette identified it when Henry paused to catch his breath and gawk a bit. "It was built to honor French soldiers who died in the Franco-Prussian War. But it was not completed until 1914, in time for us to mourn the one and a half million lost in the First World War. And now we grieve for more."

They both gazed up at its towers.

"You know, I haven't done any sightseeing here at all. I should at least see the Eiffel Tower and Notre Dame and . . . and the Louvre." He felt strange about listing the museum to Claudette, since Patsy was the reason he wanted to go.

"It opens again next week," Claudette told him. "I will take you."

For a moment he wondered if he should see her again, but only for a moment. Henry replied enthusiastically, "That's a date."

They began to walk on, but Claudette stopped. "Henri, why are you here if not to sightsee like the other American soldiers?"

He told her about Pierre, about the Lutetia.

"So, you are still the savior," she said with quiet seriousness.

Henry shook his head. "Not me, Claudette. I'm no savior. I wouldn't be alive if it weren't for Pierre, or Madame Gaulloise, or you." He kissed her hand. "And to tell you the truth, an old German soldier. He took me out to a field on orders to shoot me. I had to dig my own grave. And then . . ." Henry paused remembering how he'd put down his shovel and closed his eyes and tried to lift his soul onto the winds, like a kite, waiting for the gunshot that would end his life. "Then he just told me to go home."

"What?"

"I know. I couldn't believe it either. He told me to go

home and pointed me west. American tanks were about ten miles off. The brass always told us to try to find regular German army if we had to turn ourselves in—to save us from the SS and Gestapo. They even said some old-school officers tried to overthrow Hitler. That old sergeant who let me go wasn't a Hitler fanatic. He was clearly a World War One veteran defending the fatherland again. I think he just decided that he'd had enough killing."

For a moment, Henry remembered the soldier's sad old face. "You know," he added quietly, "I heard a deportee tell a nurse today that she had survived the march from one slave-labor camp to another because a German woman put out a trough of hot, cooked potatoes for the prisoners to take one as they passed. That woman risked a lot to do that, don't you think?"

"*Mon Dieu.*" Claudette's face flushed. "I have never considered such things possible from *les boches*. We must give thanks for your life, Henri." She led Henry into the church. They knelt before a huge mosaic of Christ with outstretched arms that glowed in the candlelight.

Claudette clasped her hands. Henry heard her whisper a prayer asking to shed her hatred. He glanced over at her in surprise. Nazis had murdered her mother and executed thirty people in her village on the word of a neighbor who accused them of feeding the *maquis* hiding nearby. He remembered well her desire to kill every Nazi she could, her calling him a fool for believing in God. "If God exists," she'd said bitterly, "how could all this happen?"

Back then, Henry had told Claudette that she must not act in revenge, that if she did, she would be as dead inside as if the Nazis shot her. But now, seeing the complete annihilation of the Vercors, the death of Madame, and the starved and haunted at the Lutetia, Henry was feeling similar rage, despite the German soldier, despite the one woman with her potatoes who'd been brave enough to be kind. He was ashamed of it but did not have the force to suppress it, not yet.

Neither he nor Claudette managed a real prayer. Within a few minutes they stood and left, Henry wondering if he'd ever completely heal that way.

Behind the basilica, Montmartre moaned with music. Claudette's mood shifted instantly upon hearing it. "Jazz is back," Claudette said, grinning, "and dancing. They were forbidden as disrespectful while the war continued. Now with victory in Europe, we can dance again. I will put on my good dress and we will go. Yes?"

Henry was game.

Claudette lived on a narrow, damp back street. Her concierge was as uninviting as the house. "Yes, but she knew how to be vague when the Gestapo searched," Claudette whispered as they climbed to the third floor. "All my friends were Resistance. My roommate made false papers. The boys down the hall worked on *Combat* with Camus."

Madame Gaulloise's Camus? "Hey, I have a book of his and—" He stopped short when Claudette tapped once, paused, and then added a sequence of: *tap . . . tap, tap-tap,* before opening the door.

"Why the signal?" Henry lowered his voice.

Claudette smiled self-consciously. "Habit. Surprise was something we did not like."

It was a tiny room with a narrow, rolled-arm couch, a cane-seat chair, and small table with one candle on it. That was it. A cracked window opened onto an alley festooned with underwear drying on lines strung up between clay pot chimneys. Henry thought of Claudette's beautiful old house and orchards in the Morvan and asked the same question she had of him: "Why are you here in Paris?"

"To be part of the change, Henri! It is our chance to change France for good. I work for the UFF, *Union des Femmes Françaises.* We print our newspaper. We speak out for jobs and equal pay for women. We demand the government provide good child care so that mothers can work and not fear for their babies. This October, the country will elect the Constituent Assembly. I campaign for the women who wish to be elected."

She pulled two jars from the cupboard. "All I have is applesauce and canned peas, oh, and prune liqueur. Would you like a little? In a few days I will queue for more. I am a J-three, between fifteen and twenty-one years of age. I am granted four eggs a month and three hundred fifty grams of bread a day, plus all the turnips and rutabagas I can carry away, so I am not bad off. They want young people to regain strength. We have much work to do!" she echoed *le patron*.

Tap . . . tap, tap-tap. Claudette's roommate entered.

"Giselle." Claudette nearly hopped up and down. "This is Henri! The flier I told you about. The man who saved my life! He is alive. Can you believe?"

The roommate eyed Henry. She did not smile. Unlike the vivacious Claudette, this girl's personality was as thin as her frame. She'd survived the war, but clearly just barely. Mechanically, she held out her hand to shake Henry's.

Claudette made Old World introductions: "Henri, this is Giselle Balmain. Giselle, this is Henri . . . " She stopped. "*Ça alors!* Henri, I do not know your last name!"

Claudette recruited five more from their floor to join her celebration. The young men were cold to Henry at first, until Claudette told of Henry's repairing cars and fusing plastique explosives at the *maquis* camp. Then the Frenchmen opened up and talked about the battle for Paris, the difficulty in finding petrol to make Molotov cocktails to hurl at German tanks. "Empty wine bottles to put the petrol in? They were simple to find," they joked. They teased one friend who said he was too tired to dance because he pedaled a stationary bike for hours each day to charge a generator that ran hair dryers in a hair salon. Shrugging good-naturedly, the man told them they should all be so lucky as to find work, especially work surrounded by beautiful women.

The group traveled from café to cabaret, collecting more friends as they went. They avoided the places they knew for sure served cat meat as beef. The songs the chanteuses sang were throaty and bawdy. The group's conversation was loud and off-color, opinionated minidramas. They spoke with large gestures and exaggerated facial expressions, leaning close to one another to make a point, far closer than any American would tolerate. They argued hotly about the best ways to improve France's economy, to make things more equal between the classes and the sexes.

As Henry listened, he realized that most of them were very left-wing in their thoughts, probably communist, including Claudette. Were these the type of people Thurman was concerned about watching? The type of people Thurman might keep a known Nazi in tow to ferret out? Henry couldn't see how these passionate, brave young people, devoted to building a better future, could be such a threat to American interests. If Orwell's paranoia about government was right, Henry would have to be careful around the Hotel Scribe. He didn't necessarily agree with the philosophies of Claudette and her friends, but the last thing he'd want to do is somehow bring the scrutiny of Thurman and his agents down on these youths. They'd had to watch their backs enough already.

As the night raced on, Henry tired of politics and focused on Claudette. While the others grew tipsy on the watered-down wine or on their dreams or on the pumped-up jazz beat, Henry lost himself in her, her new *joie de vivre*. Her bitter rage, her aura of tragedy, had been replaced with high hopes. Her new spirit was intoxicating.

She pulled him onto the packed dance floor to jitter-bug to wildly fast music. They crashed into other dancers, boys grabbing her for a swing around the floor and thrusting other girls into Henry's arms and then exchanging again—a mass of happy, sweating, sashaying young people in one big dance of unencumbered rejoicing. Claudette's laugh rang out with the music and Henry realized it was the first time he had ever heard her truly laugh.

She was so free, so full of youthful joy, she tugged at his heart. When the band switched to a slow ballad, Henry gladly pulled her to him to sway in a music-sweetened embrace. The singer crooned lyrics Henry knew well— the entire Allied world knew well—and had clung to as a hope of things returning to normal when the war was won.

> *"When the lights go on again, all over the world,*
> *And the boys are home again all over the world,*
> *And rain or snow is all that may fall from the skies*
> *above,*
> *A kiss won't mean 'Good-bye' but 'Hello to love.'"*

Claudette looked up at him with those cat-amber eyes. He couldn't take his own away from them.

As they left the dance hall, an accordion player waved at them, winked, and began singing a World War I song Henry recognized from childhood:

> *"How ya gonna keep 'em down on the farm*
> *After they've seen Paree? . . .*
> *They'll never want to see a rake or plow,*
> *And who the deuce can parleyvous a cow?*
> *How ya gonna keep 'em down on the farm,*
> *After they've seen Paree?"*

Henry left Claudette right before dawn, with the promise to rendezvous that night. He whistled the accordion player's song as he made the long walk to the Lutetia and wondered: How indeed could he return to the farm, to

shoveling chicken manure, after all this? Could he return
to Patsy?

The sun had risen by the time Henry reached the Lutetia.
He dreaded going inside to the DDT, to the legions of
sick and lost. He made his way to the board first, almost
absentmindedly, because so many days had passed with no
mark made on the note to Pierre.

Henry did a double take before sprinting inside.

Pierre's note was gone.

Chapter Twenty-five

"No, *monsieur*, I did not take down the note." Madame Zlatin tried to calm Henry. "Probably the boy took it."

Henry kicked himself—what an idiot he had been, larking around with Claudette. He should have been at the Lutetia. He should have been watching. And what was he doing there still? He should be on the streets looking for a small figure clutching a scrap of paper. He turned to run, but her words held him. "If Pierre has taken the note, he may come to me later today. If he does not, I will post it again."

"But why would he not come in?"

"He may be afraid someone wants to send him back home. Or"—she patted Henry's arm, ensuring that he stay still—"he may be afraid that we have news of his mother that is not good. These children sometimes create a fantasy to keep their hope alive. Yesterday a little girl told us with great certainty that her mother had not come yet because she had amnesia and was living as a countess in Hungary. That was her answer when a friend who survived Auschwitz told us the mother had perished.

"Wait here. A number of women came in this morning from Ravensbruck. We are processing them now. One of my assistants may have found someone who knew a Dubois. I will talk with her."

The look on Henry's face begged her to let him follow.

"No," Madame Zlatin answered before he verbalized the request. "It will be easier if it is just me. Sit. Wait."

Henry parked himself in the hotel's main lobby and tried to keep his chair from hopping down the hallway from the impatient tapping of his foot. He made himself study the mosaic ship pressed into the floor with artistically arranged chips of pink, gold, and black marble. Themes of plenty and good fortune were everywhere in the elegant Art Deco hotel. Just below the vaulted ceilings, molded in plaster, ran a lavish grapevine, cascading with plump grape bunches. The staircase leading to the rooms upstairs was lit by sunshine spilling golden through stained-glass windows cut in sunflower bursts that were outlined in thin rays of lead, haloed disc upon disc, like crowded fields of enormous blossoms. The lacework of wrought iron balconies overhanging the lobby was formed into gentle waves lapping other emblems of ships.

Henry wondered if the deportees noticed the hotel's symbols of calm waters and good harvests. He wondered if they could feel that their journey through the hurricane of human hatred and cruelty was coming to an end in a safe port. He wondered if they had nightmares, too. How long would it take for them to feel saved? A year? A lifetime?

Henry popped up and paced. Sat down. Paced again. This was as bad as sitting on the runway all prepped for mission takeoff, only to be held back for hours because of cloud cover.

Finally, one of Madame Zlatin's assistants approached, her shadow stretching long across the floor's scrubbed zigzags of gray and white marble rectangles. She was crying. It was unusual for one of the workers to weep, surrounded even as they were by tears.

Henry felt cold. "Where is Madame Zlatin?"

"She mourns," the assistant told him, her voice trembling. "A man has recognized her husband's photograph on the boards. They were together as slave laborers at a Nazi ammunition factory. When the Russians neared, some prisoners were told they would chop wood that day. The Nazis shot them in the forest. Madame Zlatin's husband was among them." She covered her eyes with her apron. "Pardon, *monsieur*," she mumbled through the fabric. "Give me a moment."

Workers gathered around her, shaking their heads as they heard the news. Henry felt terrible. After all she had done for others, couldn't Madame Zlatin have the good fortune of her husband surviving? But fate wasn't fairminded, was it? If it were, Pierre would be safe in the Vercors with his mother now. In return for all they had suffered, these "absents" should return to awaiting, intact, healthy families. But that wasn't how it worked. With irritation and some despair, Henry thought again of the plight of Sisyphus in Madame's book. Were they all doomed to such a bleak reality—struggling to overcome only to be knocked back time and time again? Henry couldn't stand for life to be that meaningless.

He also couldn't bear waiting any longer to locate Pierre. On tiptoe, he snuck down the hall to the ballroom where nurses examined the arriving deportees.

It was the smell that hit him first—the odor of woolen clothes repeatedly soaked by rain and starting to rot, shoes caked with mud and manure, bodies wracked with dysentery that had not been washed away. The smell and the anxious what-do-they-want-from-me-now silence stopped him short. He watched a woman stroke the seat of an elegant brocade armchair before gently, slowly, lowering her ragged self into it for a nurse to listen to her chest with a stethoscope. The woman looked straight ahead, enduring yet another inspection. But her hand kept brushing the embroidered fabric of the seat. Her face was full of memory. Henry wondered if she had once been a guest of the hotel, beautiful, clean, happy.

He took a deep breath and approached the line of women to explain whom he sought. *"Pardonnez-moi, je cherche une dame qui connaît Madame Dubois?"* he said slowly and carefully.

One after another shook their head. Then one answered, "I knew Madeleine Dubois."

Henry turned. It was the woman in the brocade chair. "Oh, *madame,* I—"

The nurse held up her hand, stopping him. She slipped the stethoscope along the woman's back and listened; slid it again, listened, and again. Henry's heart pounded as he waited.

"Pas de tuberculose. Sortez par là s'il vous plait." The nurse motioned for the woman to move on. She was free of tuberculosis. She called the next absent to approach.

The woman stood and joined a line waiting for towels and directions to the showers. Henry began again. *"Madame,* I am trying to find . . ."

"I know. You seek Madeleine Dubois. I knew her well."

Knew.

"Did she survive?" Henry asked in a hushed voice, already sensing death.

Sorrowfully, the woman shook her head. "The guards were lazy one day, joking and laughing. Madeleine thought she saw a chance to escape. She whispered to me that she had to return home to her son. It was madness. I tried to stop her. But she ran. The guards shot her."

Henry felt dizzy. Even though he'd had a feeling all along that Pierre's young mother had not survived, he was sick with shock and guilt. She had only been a few years older than Henry. She had died because of sheltering him. Henry could see their pretty stone cottage wrapped in climbing flowers, taste the rabbit stew and potato fritter she had fixed for him, hear her explain why she worked with the *maquis*, risking everything: Free French air for her son, no Nazi enslavement.

Well, she had won that for Pierre. But at such a price.

Henry and his pilot friends had always seen themselves as liberators. But Pierre's mother had fought just as bravely as they did—more so, perhaps, because she did her part alone, without the roar of a hundred airplane engines and guns. Henry remembered watching Pierre run to his mother, holding wildflowers he'd picked for her; she caught him up and whirled him around and around in a tight hug. Just as Lilly and he had done countless times.

Poor Pierre. He had nothing left—no family, no farm, no hometown even. All gone. Did he know?

"Madame, I think Mrs. Dubois's son may have been in the crowd outside this morning. Did a young boy approach you?"

"*Oui.*" Her eyes clouded with tears. "I am so angry with myself. What was I thinking? A child was calling out, asking for Madeleine Dubois. Without thinking I answered that she was dead. I am so sorry. The boy ran."

Henry groaned and cursed loudly enough that everyone around him stopped talking and eyed him nervously. He turned on his heel.

"*Monsieur*, wait, please." The woman reached out and grabbed his jacket, flinching as she did.

Henry glanced down at the delicate hand that held on to him and gasped a little himself. Her fingertips were swollen and red, tender. They had no nails. They'd been ripped out, probably during interrogation.

He looked up into the woman's face. It was thin but triumphant, knowing what he recognized. "It is all right, *monsieur*. They will grow back. I did not betray my friends when the Gestapo found me. Madeleine did not either. I live because of her. When I fell on our marches, she lifted me up. When she found crusts of bread in the garbage, she shared them with me. If you find her son, please tell him about the courage of his mother. Please. Perhaps bring him back to see me, Madame Latour." She let go of Henry's arm and stepped back self-consciously. "I will be clean then."

She took a towel and stepped in line for the showers.

Chapter Twenty-six

Henry bolted out of the Lutetia, into the park, looking for the marbles hustler. Surely the boy would have some idea where Pierre might hide to survive the nights. Henry didn't care if he scared him. He'd make up for it with some of those Kraft cheese slices. Heck, he'd give the boy the whole Red Cross box of provisions if he pointed Henry to Pierre. "Please, Lord," Henry prayed to himself, "help me now with my stupid French. Help me make this kid understand."

At the gate, Henry could see children playing jacks under a gum tree in the far corner of the park. He charged in, scattering them the way a dog racing into a barnyard sends panicking chickens into squawking flutters. Amid their shrieking, Henry set his targets for the hustler.

Scooping up his jacks, the boy didn't make a run for it

until Henry was almost on him. He dodged to the left, to the right, and to the left again, eluding Henry's grab. Henry heard him laugh as he darted past.

A voice like Clayton's came out of Henry. "Laugh at me, will ya?" He sprinted. Henry had run track. He was lithe and quick. He reassured himself that the boy couldn't possibly outrun him.

But the hustler was fast, making it out of the park and down the street before Henry could nab him.

Henry ran harder, realizing the boy was half a block ahead of him and could turn a corner and disappear before Henry made the street. The boy could also shimmy in between people clogging the sidewalk, while Henry, as an adult, kept knocking into them.

"*Pardonnez-moi.* Pardon. *Va!* MOVE!" Henry shouted. The boy was expanding his lead.

Henry stretched his legs longer. Pumped his arms harder. He took in deep breaths to ease the stitch he was getting in his side from his bad rib.

"Please. Out of my way!" Henry craned his neck to keep his quarry in view. He was losing him.

The boy raced up a large boulevard and then, way in the distance, veered onto a smaller street.

I saw that, kid. Can't outfox me. Henry made note of the sign in case he had to double back—rue d'Assas.

Fewer people jammed this street. Henry opened up.

He was getting closer. He could see the boy checking back over his shoulder. Just a few more yards, he'd get him. Then Henry realized the hustler was heading into an enormous park, thick with hedgerows. The boy could slip into that forest of bushes and disappear, like a rabbit went underground back to safety when chased. He'd lose the boy for sure.

Henry threw himself forward, his feet skidding on the pebbled walkways. "Stop! *Arrête!*"

The boy dove into a thicket of huge rhododendron bushes, sending the magnolia-like blossoms flying. Henry hurled himself in as well, swimming through branches, just grabbing ankle. "Gotcha!" Henry cried triumphantly.

The boy kicked Henry in the face.

Hell's bells! Henry saw stars.

The boy winnowed through more branches, then snaked along the ground underneath them. Henry was too big to squirm through the openings the boy was squirting through. In a few seconds, the boy would be on the other side of the shrubs, running, while Henry would be stuck up in the branches.

Henry closed his eyes against the sharp sticks and lunged. *Crack, crack, crack.* He crashed through the bushes, landing on top of the boy. He wrapped his arms around the boy's calves like a football tackle.

"I won't hurt you. *Je ne te fais pas mal.*" Henry hung on

as the boy thrashed. "I need your help. *J'ai besoin de ton aide*. Pierre. *Je cherche Pierre Dubois*. The boy with the marble. Hold still! *Tiens!*"

The boy punched and kicked. Pretty soon he'd break loose. "Please, I need your help," Henry pleaded. "Where is the boy with the marble? *Où est le garçon avec la bille?*"

Still, the boy bucked. Henry was losing his grip.

"Hershey bars," he said in desperation. "K-rations. Lots of them. *Pour toi. Beaucoup*."

The boy stopped squirming. Just stopped dead. *"Oui?"* He sat up. *"Pour moi?"* He cocked his head. *"Combien?"*

So that's how it was. Henry shook his head. He should have thought about bribes before. "Big box, kid," he said, making the outline of a box in the air. *"Très beaucoup*, if"—he held up his pointer finger—"if you"—he pointed to the boy and then to himself—"help me. *Aide-moi*. Find Pierre. *Trouve Pierre*."

"D'accord." The boy nodded nonchalantly, as if the chase had never happened. He stood. He didn't ask why Henry searched for Pierre. Clearly he felt no need to protect Pierre from possible trouble.

Henry hoped Pierre didn't count on this boy for anything, as glad as he was to have struck the deal. "We go to find Pierre now?" He held up the marble to remind the boy of who Pierre was.

The boy pointed at Henry. "Stuff first," he answered.

* * *

The boy did not talk to Henry as they walked from the gardens, over the Seine River, to the Hotel Scribe. In fact, he carefully stayed a few steps behind, clearly not wanting to be seen in Henry's company. He refused to come into the Scribe and waited behind a tree across the street as Henry collected his box of food. Henry was terrified that when he came back out the boy would be gone, so he didn't take time to sort out any food tins for himself. He just grabbed the box and darted back outside with everything he had—just in time to see the boy nail a pigeon with a rock and slingshot. He stuffed the carcass in his pocket, feet sticking out.

Even with the bird in his coat, the boy looked like he'd been given a Thanksgiving dinner when Henry showed him the American cans and packages.

"Deal? Show me where Pierre is?" Henry pushed to make sure the boy knew what Henry expected of him.

"Deeeeel," the boy answered.

Henry was smart enough to hang onto the carton, knowing that the instant he gave the boy the food, he'd be gone. But he handed him a box of raisins. Within a minute it was empty.

This time the boy led. When Henry tailed him too closely, he'd stop and frown, pointing back. Henry kept himself about six paces behind. Several times the boy paused in front of tailor shops, peering into the window and then backing up to stare some more. He pulled out a scrap of paper and a pencil nub to write down the addresses. Henry figured the boy was already planning some purchase with the money he'd make selling the food. But he could do that on his own time. "Hey kid, I am in a hurry. *Vite!*"

The boy looked at him with sass and dawdled extra long in front of that store. When he started walking again it was definitely at a slower pace. "Okay, okay, I get it—your way or no way," Henry muttered.

The boy didn't pick up the pace again until they came to the Louvre. There, he looked all around before pulling up some leeks planted thickly within the outlines of what clearly were usually formal flower gardens. He stuffed the vegetables into his pants pockets and took off at a jog, hissing *"Vite!"* at Henry. Remembering the man jailed in Lyon for picking his neighbor's carrots, Henry ran, jostling the contents of his box around noisily. He only vaguely wondered to whom the leeks rightfully belonged. Henry realized with some dismay how trivial the right-and-wrong of small things was becoming to him in France. That was something that would have to stop once he returned home.

They crossed back over the Seine by Notre Dame and descended to a cobblestone promenade that ran alongside the gray-green waters. It hadn't rained—Henry knew the French were worrying a drought would worsen their food situation—so the river was low, slow, and full of bad smells. Passing men fishing, Henry wondered about the safety of the catch they might eat from those waters. Two boys were very excited by the boot they'd managed to fish out.

They passed ramshackle houseboats—flat barges, covered with laundry and barking dogs. From one, a man with a reddish, blousy shirt and shaggy black hair shouted at the boy, *"Où étais-tu?"* The boy waved him off and gestured at Henry. Since he was concerned where the boy had been, perhaps the man was his father, or a guardian of some kind. Henry made note of the boat in case he needed to find the boy again.

Finally, after going under a bridge where a number of hobos slept on bundles, they came to a narrow strip of green beside the river. Between the street lamps ran a row of double benches, back to back. The peaks between several of them were covered with cardboard and newspapers, creating a shelter just big enough for a child.

"Voilà!" The boy waved at the benches and grabbed at the box. Henry held on to it for a moment longer. He told the boy his name, *"Je m'appelle Henri Forester,"* in case he ever needed help. He asked the boy his name: *"Comment t'appelles-tu?"*

The boy eyed him suspiciously and then grinned. "Charles de Gaulle." He yanked the box out of Henry's grasp and hurried away.

Henry watched him go. *Sure, kid, General de Gaulle.* Then, heart pounding, Henry crept close to the first little house of cards.

Chapter Twenty-seven

Two pairs of feet in shoes cut open so that toes could grow poked out from under the cardboard. Silently, barely breathing, Henry inched toward the open edge of the hut. Inside he could see blond curls over two virtually identical young faces pressed close together, brother and sister, like kittens asleep in a shoe box.

He tiptoed to the next teepee. Empty.

The last one smelled of cigarette smoke. Henry peeped in and caught a young teen mid-drag. *"Zut!"* The youth scrambled out the other end.

This time Henry anticipated the dash. He grabbed the youth by the collar. He couldn't understand the flood of French the youth hurled at him, it was so fast and full of foul-sounding slang. He let him go. Given this boy's attitude and the experience Henry had just had with the marbles hustler, he knew he wasn't going to get anything worthwhile out of him. The youth ran off making a rude gesture. Henry would have laughed if the youth's poverty and isolation had not been so painfully obvious.

Henry went back to the middle hut and looked in. There was a pile of marbles and a candy bar cradled in a nest of crumpled newspapers. The bedding reminded Henry of how Pierre had lined the hole in his barn wall with a blanket, a pillow, and an old rag doll to reassure the fliers he hid there. His gut told Henry this was Pierre's shelter.

But where was Pierre? Would he come back? It was strange that he hadn't taken the treasures he'd obviously won in marble games with him. Could that mean he'd given up and left the city? Or what if he had done something awful after learning his mother was dead?

Henry was overwhelmed with disappointment and worry. He buckled beside the little cardboard house and covered his face. He'd failed. For all he knew Pierre could be at the bottom of the Seine by now. American bombers had hit the Nazi ammunition factory in which Pierre's father had been forced to work and killed him. Henry's presence had probably led the Milice right to Pierre's mother. Pierre's grandfather was shot during her arrest and his mother died at Ravensbruck. Pierre's losses, his desolation, were Henry's fault.

Henry sank into a gully of regret, guilt, and frustrated tears. He had absolutely no idea what to do. He felt as lost as when he had fallen out of the sky onto Nazi-controlled France.

"Monsieur?" A gentle voice and a small hand on his shoulder made Henry jump and jerk up his head, wiping his face in embarassment. There stood a fragile and extremely fair boy with tufts of golden hair—one of the slumbering children.

"Ne vous inquiètez pas." The child spoke reassuringly and patted him. *"Vos parents reviendront."*

The boy's French was strangely accented. Henry could only understand that he offered comfort because he thought Henry was weeping over his own parents. The child tried another language, which completely flummoxed Henry. Russian maybe?

"I am sorry, I do not understand," Henry tried, almost expecting the boy to speak three languages.

The child shook his head. *"Je ne comprends pas."*

"Moi non plus," Henry allowed. He figured he'd attempt his French and hope the boy would make it through his accent better than he was getting the boy's. He told him he was looking for Pierre. Henry was a friend who wanted to help Pierre.

The boy answered something about Pierre's mother and the Hotel Lutetia.

Henry nodded. But what Henry really wanted to know was if the boy had seen Pierre *after* Madame Latour told Pierre his mother was dead. Very carefully, Henry explained that there was bad news about Pierre's mother.

"Oui, oui. Ils disent ça pour capturer les enfants." The boy's sister was suddenly standing beside him as well, explaining that adults lied to kidnap children. They had told her that their mother was dead. But they were wrong. She lived. *"C'est faux. Elle reviendra. Nous avons reçu une carte postale."* The girl showed Henry a post-card of a lake in Germany, dotted with teeny canoes and sunbathers. He couldn't translate what the mother had scribbled, but clearly the girl believed she lived because of the postcard.

Henry had heard at the Lutetia that some of the labor camps had forced prisoners to send propaganda messages home. The girl's postcard was frayed and folded, read a thousand times over, maybe a year old. With a lump in his throat, he handed it back and forced himself to smile and nod reassuringly.

Trying to keep the conversation going, he asked if Pierre had been told a lie.

"Une femme lui a dit que sa mère était morte. Il n'y croit pas."

Henry thought he would scream in frustration. He understood that Pierre did not believe his mother was dead. Where was he now, did she know?

"Il a un travail, non?" the boy asked his sister.

She elbowed him and frowned and did not answer.

A job? Did the boy say Pierre had a job? But before he could ask more, the sister took the brother's hand. She'd gotten wary. Henry had obviously asked too many questions. They were heading off to church, the girl said, pointedly adding her good-bye, *"Au revoir, monsieur."*

Henry clung to every ounce of self-control he had to not grab them and try to squeeze information out of them. Instead, he asked politely if he could come back to visit.

The boy smiled. The girl dragged him away.

Henry needed help—someone who could really understand these children and question them in a way that wouldn't frighten them. He couldn't ask Madame Zlatin—not on the heels of her learning that her husband was dead. Maybe Claudette would . . . *Oh Lord! Claudette!* Henry realized that he was supposed to have met her an hour ago.

As Henry reached the Place Saint-Germain-des-Prés and sprinted toward the Café des Deux Magots, he expected Claudette to be gone, tired of waiting; or, at the very best, furious with him. Instead she was on the fringes of its sidewalk tables, part of a crowd listening attentively to a handsome man with large dark eyes and combed-back wavy hair. She glowed with excitement and simply slipped her arm through Henry's to draw him near. She must be completely starstruck to not have noticed the time, thought Henry, with a little spasm of jealousy.

"*Henri, c'est formidable*," she whispered. "Before you are the leading minds of our country. Look there—that is Albert Camus, the editor of *Combat*. With him is Jean-Paul Sartre's love, Simone de Beauvoir, a very important thinker for me. She writes of women's natural abilities and right for independence."

Normally Henry would have been interested in Camus because of Madame, but he was focused on finding Pierre. He tried to pull her away. "Claudette, I need your help."

"No, no, Henri. *Une minute*. I want to hear more of what Camus says. A woman just complained of seeing so many 'cadavers' from the camps walking the streets, of reading his editorials about atrocities. She is tired of the 'rutabaga era,' of being sad. She wants to laugh again. *Mon Dieu*, how heartless." She paused, listening. "Monsieur Camus is saying that we must honor the returning absents and their struggles and create a social democracy . . ." She listened again, then translated, "governed by morality, and free of the bourgeois who let the Nazis in and whose souls are too delicate to hear such truths." She laughed outright at Camus's sarcasm when the chicly dressed woman stood up, insulted, and flounced out of the café.

"Claudette." Henry turned her around to face him. "That's what I need your help with. Pierre's mother is dead. Dead at Ravensbruck for the Resistance. I think I know where Pierre has been sleeping—down by the river near Notre Dame. There are children I can't understand who know him. Please, I need you to talk to them."

"*Oui, Henri*. But of course." Claudette took his hand.

The crowd at the restaurant was breaking up as well. One of the men Henry had met the night before approached them. He nodded at Henry before turning to Claudette. "Our returned POWs are massing at La Mutualité. Twenty-five thousand of them. They are protesting the government's neglect of them. We are all going. Come, Claudette. We need to support them."

"Twenty-five thousand. *C'est incroyable*," she muttered.

Henry tightened his grip on her hand. "I need you to help me now, Claudette."

Her friend stepped in front of Henry to block his path. He looked at Claudette with anger. "You prefer this boy to me?"

Claudette laughed lightly. She told the man he flattered himself.

Henry bristled. "Look, buddy, this doesn't concern you."

"*Mais oui*, it does." He shoved Henry.

Henry staggered a bit, but held his ground. "Back off."

The Frenchman shoved him again.

This time Henry pushed back.

"Stop it, both of you," Claudette cried. "Antoine," she said to the Frenchman, "behave yourself. This man risked his life to help liberate us."

"So. I see how it is, Claudette. You are one of those American-hunters. Will you sell yourself to him for a ticket to America and the fat-cat life?"

"Hey! That's enough, pal," Henry warned, balling up his fist for a good punch if it came to that.

But Claudette beat him to it. The explosion of her slap was so loud, a passerby *ooh-la-laa*ed.

Antoine clutched his reddening face and spat at her feet before stomping off. Claudette seemed completely unconcerned. Henry wondered if they had had similar arguments before.

"Come, Henri." She took his arm and walked them away. "What fools men are. I swear I will never marry."

"Aw, Claudette, you'll marry. The boys won't leave you alone till you do. You're too beautiful."

She stopped and looked up earnestly into his face. "No, Henri, unless they change the laws and attitudes in France, I will never marry. If I marry, my husband becomes the *chef de famille* and I am legally nothing but a child. De Gaulle is calling for four million 'handsome babies' in the next ten years to replenish our population. Women will be told to stay home and stay pregnant." She began walking again. "No, that is not for me. I am fighting for the right to work."

"It wouldn't be that bad for you in America," Henry said quietly, not really knowing what he was suggesting.

But Claudette didn't seem to hear him.

CHAPTER TWENTY-EIGHT

A sea of people followed them on the boulevard Saint Germain. "We will pass near La Mutualité, Henri. I will pause just a moment to see what happens at this demonstration. We will write about it for our UFF paper."

"Claudette, please, I really have to talk with those children before I lose them."

"I will be only a moment, Henri. It is important." Claudette was all business now.

"Okay, Claudette, five minutes. What's their beef anyway?" he asked with irritation.

"Beef?"

"Sorry. I mean, what are they mad about? And who are they?" There were thousands of bedraggled prisoners and camp survivors returning every day—Resistance fighters, political 'undesirables,' Jews, forced laborers. It was hard to keep them straight.

"These are our soldiers, captured when France fell, prisoners since 1940. Some people blame them for the Occupation and our humiliation, saying they did not fight hard enough. So they have come back to a France that is scornful of their courage, a France completely changed. So many have lost everything—their houses destroyed by Allied bombing, their families scattered as refugees, sometimes their wives taking on new loves, thinking they were dead. The government has promised them a new suit of clothes and shoes, but there are few to be had. The ministry did give them a thousand francs each as they reentered the country—but as you know that will buy next to nothing these days."

Henry calculated that to be about twenty dollars. He knew how American GIs would react to getting twenty bucks in bonus for five years of jail. All hell would break loose.

And that's what they came to—thousands upon thousands of men shaking signs that demanded clothes and shoes. They shouted angry complaints that de Gaulle's new army had beautiful new uniforms while they were in rags. Through a megaphone, someone urged the crowd to march on the home of Henri Frenay, head of the ministry for prisoners: He had betrayed them all. He crawled with Vichyists!

Claudette gasped. "Monsieur Frenay was Resistance. He helped start *Combat*. He fought for these men, for France.

How can they turn on him in this way? He is a good man."
She called out, *"Non! Frenay est bon."*

Men surrounding them glared at her. Henry could feel
the mob bubbling toward violence. "Shhhh, Claudette.
You can't stop this."

The crowd began chanting: *Frenay out, Frenay to the
stake!* It sounded like a guillotine crowd from the French
Revolution.

Claudette screamed to be heard over them, "Idiots! He
fought for you! *Il a lutté pour vous!*"

"Shut up, Claudette. You can't fight twenty-five thousand juiced-up soldiers."

"Il a lutté pour vous!" she continued shouting, ignoring
Henry.

Henry grabbed her around the waist and lifted her off
the ground to carry her out of the mob. Enraged faces
warned Henry that he had just a few seconds to get her
out of harm's way.

"Coward," she yelled at Henry, flailing at him. "Let go."

He held on. "You can't win this today, Claudette. Choose
your battles. Write about it. Write what you think in your
paper and pass it out to everyone in Paris. Screaming at
this crowd is suicide. Look at it." He grabbed her face and
turned it. "Look!"

The men were on the move. Many of them were picking up stones as they walked.

"Mon Dieu," she whispered.

Bright red caught Henry's eye. A couple of the soldiers holding signs demanding clothes were huddled with a man in a crimson shirt and a boy. He looked more closely. He was right. It was the man on the boat and the marbles hustler. The group shook hands and then looked around furtively before parting. Something was up. Henry's mind played the day back in his mind—the hustler checking out tailor shops and writing down addresses, the small boy by the river letting slip that Pierre had a "job" and his sister cutting him off. Henry suddenly remembered having heard at the Lutetia that there were a rash of break-ins happening at Paris clothes shops.

Good grief. The hustler wasn't planning on purchasing clothes. He was probably getting ready to break into a store and hawk the stuff to these soldiers. Could Pierre be involved? Was that the "job" the gentle, golden-haired boy had referred to? Could that be why his sister had been so quick to hush him?

"Come on, Claudette," Henry grabbed her hand. "We gotta follow that man and boy. I think they'll lead us to Pierre."

He and Claudette shadowed at a distance, dodging men running to join the protest. It was hard to keep the pair in sight without getting too close. When the duo looked back in their direction, Henry and Claudette had to pretend to peer in shop windows. They held hands, whis-pered in each other's ears, like a couple out for a stroll. Claudette instantly snapped back into the right playact-ing, having spent years as a lookout and a shadow for the *maquis*. Henry tried to control his impatience, his impulse to run ahead. He followed her lead just as he had when his life had depended on her.

The hustler was backtracking along the very route he and Henry had taken from the Hotel Scribe to the little encampment of cardboard shelters. He'd definitely been checking out some options. Near the Louvre, just off the Rue de Rivoli, the pair stopped in front of what once had been an elegant storefront, now run-down as all Paris was. There was a tweed suit and several hats in the window. Henry pulled Claudette into an alcove entrance.

Several men carrying clubs joined the two. "Henri," Claudette whispered, "that is trouble. I am certain those men with the sticks are looking for a collaborator. The return of the absents has been so shocking there has been a resurgence of retributions against Nazi informants and anyone suspected of being responsible for a *maquis* fight-er's arrest."

Across the street, the group argued.

"Can you hear what they are saying?" he asked Claudette.

"I think they have arrived at the same time by accident.

The men are after someone in an upstairs apartment. The pair we followed is after the clothes. Your man—the man in the red shirt—is telling them to wait, to not break down the door and make noise. He says he has a very small and agile boy who can crawl through the window and let them into the shop and the apartment." She strained to hear more. "The men like the idea that they can surprise the *collabo* so he cannot get away. They want the small boy to come with them to several houses tonight." She glanced at Henry. "The boy with them cannot do that, he is too big. They must be waiting for someone else."

Henry nodded. "I bet it's . . ."

Henry caught sight of a small figure walking up the street toward the men. Despite the passage of a year, he knew that walk. He'd never forget that small child appearing on the roadway to take his hand and lead him to safety.

"It's Pierre!" He'd found him, at last!

Filled with joy and relief, Henry started to dart across the street.

Claudette grabbed him. "Wait, Henri. Those men will not let you have Pierre. Let him do what they want first and then we can lure him away as they go upstairs." Henry tried to jerk away. Claudette persisted. "There are too many of them, Henri. Think! Listen to me. If you rush in, they will scatter, taking Pierre with them. Or worse for you. You cannot fight three men with clubs. You must believe what I tell you. It will be the same as when we went after the Nazis. We let the group go in to raid a house and then picked off those standing guard outside, one by one. Trust me."

Henry knew she was right. But what if they hurt Pierre? What if the collaborator had a gun and in self-defense shot Pierre by mistake? He was in agony.

Claudette tugged on his sleeve. "Trust me," she whispered.

Henry ground his teeth. *Two minutes, that's it; then I'm going in.*

The man in the red shirt hoisted Pierre up easily. Pierre balanced himself on the man's shoulders like a carnival act. Henry frowned. The move was practiced. How long had that jerk been taking advantage of Pierre?

Claudette noticed it, too. "Your Pierre may not want to be saved, Henri. There have been a number of burglaries in the city, taking clothes, coats, hats, and shoes. He looks like he knows exactly what to do."

Henry felt sick as Pierre pried open the window latch, lowered the sash quietly, and pulled himself into it. There was a moment of squirming and then Pierre's legs and feet disappeared. Soon he opened the tall wooden door. The group swarmed in.

"Now!" Henry and Claudette sprinted to the building and slipped into the door left ajar. The man in the red shirt, the marble hustler, and Pierre were just sneaking toward the clothes in the storefront window.

Henry lunged, shoving the man aside. "Pierre, it's me—Henri!" he cried. He held out his arms, expecting Pierre to embrace him, as he had at their good-bye.

Pierre stared at him.

Birdbrain! Henry berated himself. He was moving too fast. But there wasn't time to spare. "Pierre, don't you recognize me? It's Henri. The American. You taught me French, I taught you English. You saved my life."

Pierre blinked and stared more.

Claudette tried, telling him not to be afraid. *"Ça, c'est le pilote qui est resté chez toi dans le Vercors."* She pointed at Henry, telling Pierre he was the pilot Pierre had helped, back home in the Vercors. The one who took him to the priest for safety. Remember? *Souviens?"*

Pierre looked at her blankly.

Henry heard shuffling atop the steps, the sound of a man struggling, his cries muffled. They had to hurry. Henry tried again: "I hid you in the barn from the Milice when they came. Your *maman* asked me to . . ." That was the mistake.

At *maman*, Pierre began to back away, shaking his head.

"Henri, look out!"

From behind, the man in the red shirt jumped on Henry. Henry managed to dip and roll him off. "Take Pierre and run, Claudette!" he shouted. He grabbed the man by his crimson shirt, slammed him against the wall, and hit him as hard as he could across the jaw. He felt Claudette brush past him, could hear her coaxing Pierre to follow her; they would look for his mother together, *"Viens avec moi, chéri. Nous trouverons ta maman."* The front door swung open and they were gone.

Run, Claudette!

The vigilantes came down the stairs, shoving the blubbering collaborator with their clubs. *"Qu'est-ce qui s'est passé?"* they shouted at the man in the red shirt.

"Au secours!" He gasped for help.

Before Henry could turn to defend himself, a club hit his head. In a flash of hot splintering light and pain, Henry felt the enormous blow, and then nothing.

Chapter Twenty-nine

"Henri, wake up. Please, open your eyes."

Henry could hear a voice calling him. He struggled up through blackness, swimming through pain. *Patsy? Where are you, Pats?*

"*S'il te plaît, Henri.* Do not be dead. Look at me."

Henry forced his eyes open. There was a blurred but beautiful face over his. *Patsy, you still mad at me, girl?* Trembling, he reached out to touch a soft cheek. It was moist with tears.

"Thank God. You live." Claudette gathered Henry into her arms. "I could not bear to lose another. Not like André," she murmured to herself. "No more."

Henry struggled to place himself. André? The image of Claudette in a wheat field, sobbing, gently rocking the corpse of her beau, came to him. He concentrated on the face. Its bits and pieces slowly slid together. It was Claudette. Of course. This was France.

"Where is Pierre?" he croaked.

"Come. I must move you. Quickly."

Henry could hear blasting whistles.

"What is that?"

"The police. Come. You must get up. *Vite.*"

Claudette braced herself under his arm and pushed Henry to his feet. He staggered to the door, feeling a trickle of blood going down the back of his neck. The world reeled in front of him. "I need to sit for a minute, Claudette."

The whistle blasts were closer.

"No, Henri, you must not. We have to walk away now. Right now."

She opened the door and propelled Henry through. He felt something brush his head and reached up to swat it away—his head hurt so much as it was.

He grabbed a shoe. Henry gasped and cried out.

"Shhhh. Keep walking, Henri."

A body hung from the archway—the *collabo* had been lynched.

Henry hurried as best he could. He understood. He had to get away before the police came and thought he had something to do with the murder. Claudette half dragged him down the street and into the long gardens in front of the Louvre. She guided him to a pool ringed with statues. Dousing a handkerchief, she washed his face. She rinsed it and dabbed, rinsed and dabbed, leaving a little cloud of blood in the water each time.

After a few minutes Henry could focus his thoughts through the pounding in his head. He took her hand to stop her tending his wound. "Claudette. Where is Pierre?"

She looked away, uncharacteristically hesitant. "I lost him, Henri."

"Damn it!" Henry slammed his hand on the marble pool, then held his head against the throbbing he'd caused.

"I am so sorry, Henri. Please, please, forgive me." She gathered him into her arms again and refused to let go when he tried to wrench away. "Listen to me. He pulled away from me. I chased him down the street. For a moment, I had him cornered. I told him that if he came to the Hotel Lutetia tomorrow morning, we would take him to his mother."

Henry made a face at the deception.

"I know, Henri. But I could think of no other way."

"Do you think he believed you?"

She paused. "I think he called me a liar. He spoke so quietly, I am not sure. He looked at me with those huge, solemn eyes." Henry remembered those eyes, like those of an old man sometimes. Claudette continued, "But he nodded before he ran away. I am sorry to not do better, Henri. I will help you to the hotel. And I will keep watch with you."

Under the stars, in the garden across from the Lutetia, they sat through the night. Even though it was early June, the night air chilled. Henry borrowed a blanket from inside, and wrapped himself and Claudette together in it. She tucked her legs up under her skirt and rested against his chest, content, unusually quiet. His head began to clear.

"Claudette?"

"*Oui?*"

"I have a book by your Camus that I cannot understand. Maybe you can explain it to me, because Madame Gaulloise seemed to think it was important that I get it."

"I will try, Henri. Camus is a great man. He rallied Paris to resist the Nazis."

"Have you read the *The Myth of Sisyphus?*"

"*Oui.*"

"Please explain that to me. It's so irritating—his having to push a rock up a hill for eternity."

Claudette sat up to look at him. "You are such an American," she teased. "Your countrymen think they can fix everything, that all battles can be won."

Henry bit his tongue to keep from snapping at her. Hadn't they fixed Europe? The French would still be occupied without the Allies. But then he thought about all the destruction left by American bombs, about how the French had saved his skin, and kept silent.

"Sisyphus is the absurd hero," Claudette continued.

"Right. Is being absurd good?" he asked.

Claudette laughed. "You miss the point, Henri. There is no sun without shadow. Camus says that the greatness of man lies in his decision to be stronger than his condition. Sisyphus is superior to his fate because he scorns it. Sisyphus could choose suicide because his existence is meaningless, but instead the struggle becomes his meaning. 'The struggle itself toward the heights is enough to fill a man's heart.'" She repeated the sentence Madame Gaulloise had quoted, then swept her hand out toward the garden and the Lutetia. "Given all we survived, all that is left to do, it is a good philosophy, no?"

Slowly, Henry nodded. He understood. Madame had survived Ravensbruck because she could find within herself an impenetrable fortress of purpose, of righteous scorn for those who would seek to destroy humanity, a stubborn *joie de vivre*—no matter what the Nazis did to her, no matter what her fate ultimately was. She must have hoped the book would tell Henry that he had to find answers in his own soul.

Henry was struck with another recognition. Patsy had tried to tell him something like that when she said she was afraid she would not be enough for him—that she couldn't fix things for him, that she frightened her. His mind flew home. *You don't need to be afraid now, Pats. I'm better. I'm stronger. I can fight my demons. I'll follow the example of Madame,* le patron, *Claudette, and yes, even Pierre.*

Finding Pierre, taking him into Henry's home to save him just as Pierre had saved Henry, would let Henry shed much of his guilt and sorrow and begin anew. Lilly was right—helping someone else, shaking a fist at fate even, would help him stand tall again. He knew the nightmares, the regrets, would still visit him, but he would know them for what they were—scars healing slow and every once in a while breaking open again. He'd finally negotiated his peace.

Claudette snuggled back against his heart. "Henri?"

"Yes?"

"I cannot go to America with you."

Henry caught his breath. So she had heard him earlier. He started to apologize. He wasn't sure what he meant by it. He loved Patsy, and yet . . .

"We live because of one another, Henri," Claudette stopped him. "Yet we cannot live *with* one another. My country is no longer your fight. It is mine." Her voice was trailing off. "But I will always treasure you," she murmured. "You are the handsome flier who helped me find my way."

A few minutes later, she was asleep.

Henry dozed a little himself. Dawn woke him. He gently laid Claudette down on the bench and went to the garden's gate to watch for Pierre. As he passed, he looked over to the statue of the three women of kindness.

He froze. From behind the carved robes of the stone mother cradling her infant peeked out a small, very dirty, human hand. Henry tiptoed closer. A boy had nested himself up against the back of the statue. Henry stood on his toes to see the face.

It was Pierre.

Henry dropped to his knees, trying to squelch his instinct to jump on Pierre and hog-tie him until he could talk some sense into him. But that wasn't right. Pierre had to decide to come to Henry himself. But how? Pierre had not even seemed to recognize him yesterday.

Ever so quietly, Henry eased himself down on the steps beside Pierre. Seeing him on the stark white stone reminded Henry of leaving Pierre at the church—tucking him into the starched, bleached covers of the bed in the priest's sparse white room. That night Henry had done the only thing he could think of to comfort Pierre. He had sung the song Lilly always put him to bed with when he was young, "You Are My Sunshine," and then given him that lucky marble.

Henry pulled the marble from his jacket pocket. The marble had represented his ability to triumph. It had been his connection to home, to safety, when he was fighting in a burning sky over Europe. When he'd given it to Pierre almost a year ago—when Pierre's mother was arrested and Henry had to continue on his escape—Henry had hoped that the marble would lend the boy some of Henry's new-won strength. He wanted Pierre to have it as proof that Henry cared about him and would be there for Pierre as well—if Henry survived.

Well, he had survived. And now he was here. It was his turn to help. Henry hoped the marble would somehow remind Pierre of all that.

Henry replicated the circumstances of their good-bye as best he could. He started singing—low, soft—the ballad about how much joy one person could bring another in troubled times: *"You are my sunshine, my only sunshine, you make me happy when skies are gray. . . ."*

Pierre's eyes fluttered open.

Henry kept singing and rolled the marble, that cloud of luck, toward Pierre. *"Henri avec Pierre. Toujours.* Wherever I go you are always with me."

Pierre kept his cheek on the granite as the marble rolled to a stop in front of his nose.

"Henri avec Pierre," Henry whispered again. *Come on, Pierre, trust me.*

"Ma bille. Mon nuage."

Henry caught his breath at the sound of Pierre's voice, so familiar, yet so different in its sorrow. Pierre had always had a lightness, a hope, about him, even in the middle of his country's devastation, his family's danger. "Yes, your marble, Pierre. Your cloud."

"Bonne chance."

"That's right. *Oui.* It was to bring good luck."

"*Ça n'a pas marché.*" Pierre answered flatly that it did not do so.

Henry winced. No, Pierre was right. The marble did not bring him good luck. In fact, the past year had brought Pierre nothing but tragedy. Henry thought a moment. "But it did bring good luck in a way, Pierre. I found you because of this marble. I don't know that I would have without it."

"*Vous me cherchiez?* Look? Me?"

"Yes, I have searched for you. Just as you looked for me on the road and took me to safety, to *tranquillité.*"

Tears filled Pierre's eyes. "*Ma maman est morte?* Dead?"

Henry hesitated to answer the blunt question. But trust required honesty. If Pierre bolted, he'd just have to run after him and try something else. "Yes, your mother is dead."

Pierre closed his eyes. His tears splashed on the stone.

Henry didn't move, barely breathed, waiting.

Pierre opened his eyes again. Slowly, carefully, he reached for the marble. "*Henri avec Pierre? Toujours?*"

"*Toujours.*" Henry's voice cracked. "Always."

Pierre closed his hand around the marble and looked up at Henry. "*Tranquille?*" he whispered.

"Yes, Pierre. Safe. *Tranquille avec moi.* From now on." Henry took his hand. "Let's go home."

have a swimming hole in one of the creeks feeding the James, where it pools quiet. A big willow hangs over a bank of soft moss and there's a tire swing and . . ." Henry realized that Pierre couldn't follow all that. "You'll see. *La rivière est belle.*"

The swimming hole was Henry's favorite place. His happiest hours had been down there, splashing around with Patsy. It'd been where he'd first kissed her before leaving for France. His heart did a little skip as he thought of her dimpled smile.

Henry sighed, wondering if Patsy was as nervous as he was to see her again. He'd phoned from New York City when they arrived to tell Clayton and Lilly they were coming so they'd be ready for Pierre. Lilly was thrilled. Clayton had muttered that at least Henry'd be home in time to pick the string bean field. Typical. Just as long as Clayton was nice to Pierre.

But he hadn't been able to call Patsy. Her family didn't have a telephone. The train would get them to Richmond before a letter could arrive. So Henry had asked Lilly to tell Patsy that he was coming home to her and that some-day he wanted to show her Paris. It was a beautiful city for a beautiful girl.

Hopefully, Patsy wouldn't ask him how he arranged the boat trip home since the ship passage back had been Claudette's doing. Henry wasn't so sure he wanted to discuss Claudette with Patsy. Not that he had anything to hide; it was just . . . complicated. He and Claudette had no future together. He didn't want one either. But what they had had was sacred and between them—they were war buddies almost, survivors of the same shipwreck.

He smiled thinking of Claudette. Although he had left her in a troubled land, Claudette was strong and ready to take on postwar France. In fact, God help anyone getting in her way! Through her UFF connections, Claudette had found them a berth on a Soviet boat to Norway. Once there, no one understood a word Henry was saying and he let his remaining money speak for him and Pierre. Henry was pretty certain that the emigration papers she came up with for Pierre were forged—since that's what her friends had done for the Resistance.

But he wasn't going to ask questions. The lines of right and wrong were still forming in postwar France. Given what he'd witnessed and heard of, slipping one small boy in need of a home out of it seemed small pota-toes. There were so many children in need, surely no one would care that one was being helped in a less than official way. Besides, given his worry that Thurman still shadowed him somehow, Henry didn't want to force his way through proper channels that might alert the OSS man of his taking Pierre to Virginia. That seemed just too good a piece of blackmail. If Thurman got hold of that information and push came to shove, it'd be mighty hard for Henry to not give up a name or two of his *maquis* friends. So he and Pierre left Paris as soon as they could.

Henry and Claudette said their good-byes at the Louvre. She'd taken him on the way to the train station, just as she promised. The *Mona Lisa* had just been put back on the wall. The curators had evacuated her and driven her around in a humidity-controlled ambulance to escape capture by Hitler. Her eyes really did follow Henry around the room, just like Patsy said.

Claudette also showed Henry some Picasso paintings. "He lives in Paris, you know. The symbolism in his cubist work is wonderful, no?" Claudette murmured more to herself than to Henry.

Picasso. Madame Gaulloise had sold her Picasso painting to finance his escape and that of some Jewish musicians. Gazing at the painted jumble of body parts and geometric figures, and then at the fiery, idealistic Claudette, Henry recognized what kindred souls she and Madame Gaulloise were; it was as if Claudette was Madame's spiritual daughter.

Henry opened his bag and pulled out Madame's scarf. Madame had said to give it to Lilly. But Henry could see that it should stay in France with Claudette. She would carry the flame of Madame's compassion and courage forward with her own. As he wrapped the deep green silk around her neck, Henry told Claudette who it had belonged to and why she should have it. He added that if she ever met Picasso to tell him about Madame.

"Wear this scarf when you run for president, Claudette."

"Henri, c'est bien la maison? Home?"

"Yes, home." Henry was relieved for Pierre's sake that they were arriving in early July when the house was still pretty. By the end of the month, the sun would have scorched things brown. Right now the cedars along the drive were still green and fresh. The two oaks by their Victorian farmhouse spread out a cool shade on the clover. Lilly's nasturtiums and marigolds were bright and full—happy lines of orange, gold, and red marching from the drive to the front door.

Just like his last homecoming, the first to greet the taxi was good old Speed, wet and sloppy from the creek, wagging his entire body in a friendly hello. When Henry opened Pierre's taxi door, Speed coaxed him out with a big, slurping dog kiss.

"Henry!" Lilly ran out of the kitchen, screen door slamming, wiping her hands on her apron. Henry hugged her, catching the scent of apples and cinnamon—somehow she always smelled of warm things baking in the oven. "Ma, did you make a pie for me?"

"Of course, honey. Today's the Fourth. You're home. We need to celebrate."

Henry had no present for Lilly, having given Madame's scarf to Claudette. Outside the Louvre a man was doling out fistfuls of a fancy perfume, Chanel No. 5, to passing GIs, telling them to take it home to their girls. But Claudette had snatched the bottle away and smashed it on the ground, saying that Coco Chanel had been a *collabo*, living at the Ritz with an Abwehr spy, and was just trying to buy her way out of a trial by bribing Americans with perfume.

"Ma, I'm sorry," Henry apologized to Lilly. "I was so short on money. You wouldn't believe what food cost. So I couldn't buy anything nice for you." But he did plan to show her that lily of the valley he'd pressed into Madame's book and to try to find some seeds for the flowers. Lilly would love them planted under the oaks.

"Pshaw, sugar. You're home," Lilly looked up into his face. "You look well and whole. What more could I want, son?"

She turned to Pierre, who was hanging on to Speed like a shield. "And," she said, smiling her welcome, "you have brought me a new friend." She took Pierre's hand to shake it and said, *"Bienvenue à ta nouvelle maison."* Lilly's drawl mangled the French, but her words pulled a tiny return smile out of Pierre. She even kissed him on each cheek in proper French style.

"Ma, where'd you learn that?"

She winked. "I have my ways."

"That the boy?" Clayton stood behind them, a bucket of eggs beside him. Gruff, as always.

Henry stiffened. "Yes, Dad, this is *Pierre*." The first thing he was going to make sure of was that Clayton never referred to Pierre as "boy," the way he'd always minimized Henry.

But Pierre seemed to understand Clayton immediately. Perhaps he reminded Pierre of his own cantankerous grandfather. *"Vos oeufs sont beaux, monsieur,"* he said, pointing to the bucket of eggs. *"Vous devez bien prendre soin de vos poules."*

Henry laughed. *Smart kid.* Pierre obviously knew about catching flies with honey. Clayton would definitely respond well to a compliment about his farming.

"What did the boy say?" Clayton asked.

"Pierre said that since you have so many nice eggs, you must take good care of your hens. I told you he came from a farm, Dad."

"Hmphf. Well, pay the cab. Welcome home, son."

"Where's Patsy, Ma?" he asked Lilly as they entered the house.

"She'll be here for the picnic in just a little while, sugar. She's working at Miller and Rhodes for the summer, in the ladies' section. There was a big sale yesterday and she didn't get home till late. So she's helping her mother cook. She said to tell you that she can hardly wait to see you. She's had good news while you were gone, Henry. She received a full scholarship to Sweet Briar College." Lilly slipped her arm through Henry's and said pointedly, "You know, honey, Sweet Briar is only one train stop from UVA. There's talk about a GI bill making it easy for veterans to go to college. You promised to go on to college once you got back from the war. You've already been accepted, remember?"

But all Henry heard was that Patsy was going away. His heart sank. He'd always known Patsy was smart, but he hadn't ever considered *her* going away to college. Henry caught himself. He could just imagine what Claudette would say to him if she knew he was surprised by a girl going to college. It'd blister his ear! He'd have to act happy for Patsy. She deserved that chance. Still, he couldn't help worrying about what that meant for the two of them.

If only Lilly's matchmaking could make everything right between him and Patsy. But if Henry had learned anything on this trip, it was that life was full of surprises and that he had to face up to certain things on his own.

During the picnic, Henry had two shadows, Pierre and Speed. The three of them sat wedged together on the front steps with Patsy. She and Henry held hands and smiled at one another nervously. Silently, Pierre watched them.

Henry was torn between hovering over Pierre and try-ing to steal a few moments alone with Patsy. He had so much to tell her. "Want to try the stilts?" Henry pointed to Patsy's younger brothers who were walking around the lawn on the elevated sticks.

Pierre shook his head.

"Do you want some more pie, honey?" Patsy asked him. "Pie?" she pointed to the crumbs left on the plate beside Pierre and smiled encouragingly.

He shook his head.

Henry and Patsy sighed at the same time, then blushed, then laughed at each other. The jittery anticipation and energy between them could turn on a lightbulb, Henry thought.

Pierre sighed, too, trying to be part of whatever was going on between them.

Poor kid. Henry ruffled Pierre's hair. At least dinner had gone over well. Pierre had inhaled the deviled eggs, fried drumsticks, and pie. He'd picked at the baked beans though, reminding Henry of how he'd balked at some of the French dishes he'd been given, like the moldy blue cheese. But Speed had figured out that Pierre was good for leftover scraps, so they were now buddies for life.

Still, Pierre had hardly spoken. It was going to take him a while, a few months, maybe more, to adjust.

They would all need to accept that. Henry wasn't worried about Lilly understanding. She had set up a cot for Pierre in the third bedroom that she used for sewing and farm files. She'd put him there instead of with Henry, she said, figuring Henry might wake Pierre up with . . . she paused . . . with snoring.

Henry knew what she really meant. "I'm not having those nightmares as much anymore, Ma. But even when I do, I can ease myself down. Just takes a few minutes— but I beat them back. God knows I saw a lot of things to spark nightmares over in France. I'm not ready to talk about all that today. But soon. It'll help you and Dad understand Pierre better. And I promised someone to make sure Americans *really* understand what Hitler did, how he exterminated and tortured millions of people. Millions, Ma."

Lilly nodded. "Don't tell me anything until you are ready, honey."

Henry wished he'd inherited Lilly's patience. He thought he would strangle someone soon if he couldn't get Patsy to himself. Again, he looked at her with longing and smiled.

She smiled back.

Ka-bang! Pop-pop-pop!

Patsy's brothers set off a string of cherry bombs, whooping and hollering at the Independence Day specials.

Henry jumped, startled. Deep in his mind, he heard an echo of machine-gun fire, *rat-tat-tat*, but it was only a momentary burst, like heat lightning and thunder of a receding storm.

Did you think I would allow you to escape?

Henry looked around at all the faces he loved best and pushed the ghost away. *I beat you, you SOB. I'm home.*

Henry turned to Pierre to explain the Fourth of July tradition. But then he saw the expression on Pierre's face. Pierre was terrified, shaking all over.

"You, boys," Clayton barked. "That's enough. Go on home now with those noisemakers! Want to stop my hens from laying?" Henry could tell the move wasn't Clayton's usual fun-spoiling. He was watching Pierre as well.

Patsy stood to shoo off her brothers.

Henry put his hand on Pierre's shoulder to help steady him. "It's all right, Pierre. Ease down," he spoke softly. "I know what you're thinking. But there are no Nazis here. You're safe. *Tranquille.* Look at me. *Regarde-moi.*"

Pierre looked. Those huge solemn eyes looked through Henry, seeing other things, other places. But slowly, the focus came to Henry's face. Slowly, he stopped trembling.

Lilly stood in the kitchen door, watching. There were tears on her face. She nodded at Henry, knowing. "We shouldn't take him to the fireworks," she said. "Next year.

Then he will really enjoy them." She turned to Patsy to suggest the party should end, but Patsy was already preparing to follow her brothers home.

Henry caught her up in a good-bye hug. She whispered in his ear, "Come over later. After we get home from watching the fireworks, okay?"

"You got it," Henry promised.

Clayton was still watching Pierre. Squinty-eyed, he twisted his mouth around. Henry knew that look. It meant Clayton was chewing on some thought. "You play marbles, boy?"

It was the one game Clayton had ever played with Henry and the only thing Henry had ever beaten his dad at. Given the stash of marbles Henry had seen under Pierre's bench in Paris, he'd bet good money that Pierre would take Clayton to the cleaners. What better way for Pierre to earn some respect fast from the old man?

Henry looked down at Pierre and asked him. *"Joues aux billes avec mon père?"*

A little glimmer came to Pierre eyes and he pulled their lucky marble from his pocket. He asked Henry if he really should.

"Oh yeah." Henry grinned. "For sure. *C'est une idée superbe!"* Henry turned to Clayton. "Yes, *Pierre* plays marbles."

★ ★ ★

An hour later, after Pierre had won a pile of marbles, Clayton called it quits.

Worried that being skunked by a nine-year-old would annoy Clayton, Henry softened Pierre's victory: "It's a lucky shooter, Dad."

"Naw." Clayton stuck out his lower lip, considering the match. "It was skill. Wasn't that the shooter you won off me?"

Henry was stunned that Clayton recognized it. "You know, Dad, I carried that marble with me on my missions, for good luck. It was a way to tie me to home."

Clayton swallowed hard, blinked, and rubbed his nose. "Yeah?" He kept looking forward.

"Yeah."

Clayton cleared his throat. "Come on out to the barn. I've got something to show you."

Henry followed Clayton, figuring he was in for a lecture about a new plow or a show-and-tell about some tractor he'd rehabilitated. An ace mechanic, Clayton could make any old piece of junk hum. He'd taught Henry a lot, he'd have to admit. Henry would try to listen.

The sun was setting, spilling rosy light along the grass. Swallows darted, swooped, climbed, pirouetted in the air chasing bugs—the prettiest hunters of the earth. A mother quail called her babies in to shelter for the night.

"Bob-white," she whistled. "Bob-bob-white," little voices answered. It sure was good to be home.

Clayton hurled his weight against the large sliding door that opened up almost the entire wall of the barn. Henry threw his shoulder into it, too, and then stepped back, wondering what in the world needed the barn opened up that much.

He caught his breath. Inside was the Curtiss Jenny biplane that he'd wrecked. But it was fixed—ready to fly again.

He couldn't help it. He hugged Clayton, hugged him hard and swung him around.

"Here now!" Clayton shrugged him off. But then he laughed and shook his head. "Darn fool thing, son, for me to bother with. But I figure you can crop dust to earn some money before you go on to college this fall. Time for you to go. Your mother and I will keep the boy. He looks like he knows a thing or two about farms."

"You can't overwork him, Dad, not like . . ." Henry stopped himself from criticizing Clayton for how hard he'd worked Henry. "Not like we had to do in the Depression, Dad."

"No. He needs some healing time. Your Ma says so. You can help me harvest the corn before you go off."

They stood silently, gazing together at the gleaming flying machine. Clayton was the one to break the silence.

"You know, I kind of liked working on it. I liked the sound her struts made when the wind caught them."

Henry grinned. Well, the old man wasn't such a stone after all. "You want to go up with me, Dad?"

Clayton turned to Henry. "Not me, son. I get why flying means so much to you. But it's not for me. Each man has something that keeps him aloft. For me, it's your mother." He crossed his arms and very slowly, making sure Henry followed his gaze, Clayton looked across the fields toward Patsy's farm. Then he clapped Henry's shoulder and walked back to the house, calling over his shoulder that he and Lilly would get Pierre to bed.

Laughing, lighthearted, Henry lit out across the fields. He felt his heart lift, catching the wind. He was ready to begin again, to take flight once more.

He reached Patsy's house just as her brothers were tumbling in the door, shouting about the colors and the noise of the fireworks display. He said a quick, barely polite hello to her parents. Then Henry grabbed Patsy's hands to pull her away, past the square of lights cast through the house windows onto the grass, where their feet kicked up the scent of twilight dew.

He handed her the only gift he'd been able to purchase, a book of postcards of paintings in the Louvre. He pointed to the one of *Mona Lisa*. "Her eyes do follow you around the room, Pats, just like you said." He kissed her gently. "Just like my eyes will always follow you." He stopped himself from adding, "if you will let me." That kind of question, about their future together, needed to wait a little, until they were both ready. But he did have another one.

"I have something to ask you," he said.

Patsy pulled in her breath, sharp. He could feel her hands begin to tremble ever so slightly. "Yes? I'm ready."

"Dance the skies with me?"

For just a moment, disappointment shadowed her beautiful freckled face. That wasn't the question she'd expected. But then a small smile slid onto Patsy's lips and grew into a radiant grin, that tomboy grin Henry had always loved. "Wait? Are you serious? Go up in that plane your dad rigged?"

"Yeah. Wanna?"

"I've never been in a plane before, Henry," she whispered, breathy, awed with the idea.

"I know. Wanna come?"

She nodded, bouncing on her tiptoes.

"Grab a sweater. It's cold in the clouds."

Patsy darted away and back, beaming.

Henry clasped her hand and they ran, shouting, rejoicing, falling down and pulling one another up to skip on, like children.

★ ★ ★

On laughter-silvered wings, topping the windswept
heights, Henry showed Patsy how to touch the face of
God.

AFTERWORD

*"There is no sun without shadow, and it is
essential to know the night . . . The struggle itself toward
the heights is enough to fill a man's heart."*
—Albert Camus

War ends, and the battle for peace begins.

Nations must establish true, cooperative treaties with former enemies. New governments must be formed among competing political ideologies and leaders more accustomed to fighting than negotiating. Cities, railways, ports, bridges, schools, and hospitals must be rebuilt. Farms, long neglected or destroyed, must be replanted. Banks must be replenished and reopened.

Survivors must find loved ones lost during panicked flight from oncoming armies, nurse the wounded or starved back to health, and bury their dead. Returning soldiers must ease down from battle readiness, shedding the quick-flash aggression that kept them alive under fire. They must accept what they have done and seen. War criminals must be tried in a civilized, judicial court. Lesser criminals—the weak, the passive, the followers—must be pardoned and left alone.

These are tall orders for countries and individuals alike. The hatred, suspicion, and bitter vengeance forged in the firestorms of war do not die down easily. That is especially true when a conflict is long lasting and far-flung, as was World War II.

World War II lasted six years and embroiled more than 50 nations. Death toll estimates go as high as 70 million, but the most scholarly sources estimate that a staggering 55 million people were killed, most of them civilians. In Europe alone, the Nazis methodically exterminated 14 million persons Hitler deemed "racial inferiors": Poles, Slavs, gypsies, and six million Jews.

In France, 211,000 soldiers, sailors, and airmen were lost, but so, too, were 400,000 civilians. These children, women, and men died in battle bombardments, from land mines left by Nazis, in executions, in massacres in retaliation for Resistance work, from deportation, and, tragically, in Allied bombings designed to liberate them.

France was the largest supplier of manpower and finished goods to Hitler's Germany. To win the war, the Allies had to destroy its production of ball bearings, tires, and other such items used for Nazi tanks, planes, and ships. No matter how careful Allied bomber crews were to drop their load "right in the pickle barrel," the explosions often spread beyond targeted factories, supply depots, or railway junctions. In May 1944, for instance, the Allies flew 1,284 raids over France. In one two-day period, 6,000 French persons perished.

After the war ended, five million French were left "displaced." Many were homeless refugees, their towns in ruins from the village-by-village battle for liberation. In places like Caen, for instance, only 400 of its 1,800 buildings were left standing. Others struggled to return from the concentration and labor camps to which they had been deported by Nazis and fellow Frenchmen.

Rage at French collaboration with Hitler is what continued the nation's internal strife after its liberation in late 1944. A large number of French citizens—from industrial giants to ordinary shopkeepers or small-town mayors—had willingly cooperated with the Nazis and its puppet Vichy government. Some did so because they agreed with Hitler's racism and anti-Semitism. Others cooperated because of fear or greed or a lust for power. With the help of such collaborators, 76,000 French Jews were rounded up and sent to concentration camps. A mere 3 percent survived. Also deported were 85,000 Resistance members and "political undesirables" (socialists, communists, and other radicals). Only half returned.

Most of these victims had been reported to the Nazis and the French Milice by their neighbors or coworkers, people they knew.

In retaliation for such betrayals, collaborators were attacked as D-day armies landed. In what the French called the *épuration sauvage*, "the savage purge," about 10,000 people were executed without trial. Thousands of women were shaved by mobs in punishment for their perceived romances with German soldiers. Tragically, some were *maquis* fighters who had befriended Germans in order to spy on them for the Resistance. They could not convince enraged crowds of the patriotism of their play-acting. Vigilante-style attacks escalated in 1945 as concentration camps were liberated and a tidal wave of "absents" flooded back into France—broken, emaciated, deathly sick—carrying tales of horrifying atrocities that shocked and inflamed the country.

It took incredible bravery and commitment to peace to stand for forgiveness, for healing, during this time. Yet many did. One woman, whose husband died in Buchenwald for his Resistance work, served briefly as her village's mayor and counted her largest accomplishment as being the fact that no female was shaved during her watch.

Hunger ravaged Europe. The Allies sent massive shipments of foods, but until Hitler was defeated, the majority of supplies went to troops on the front lines. Once the peace accord was signed, relief efforts began in earnest, spurred by slogans like: "Let's finish the job." In May 1945, for instance, the U.S. Air Corps flew 400 emergency flights over the Netherlands, dropping more than 800 tons of K-rations for the starving Dutch. The British also dropped tons of powdered milk, eggs, and chocolate. Church groups across the United States organized clothing drives with the same gusto American youths had scrounged old pans for scrap metal for bombs during the war. In one day a Catholic church in Richmond collected 2,416 useable garments; in a week a West Coast synagogue collected 10,000 pounds of coats.

But even with such aid coming in, the infrastructure to deliver food and clothes was nonexistent. Most French railroads, bridges, and canals were destroyed. Coal had to be mined to run what trains were working, but there was nothing to transport the coal to the stations.

In this void, some seized the opportunity to make fortunes selling food and stolen Allied goods on the black market. Sometimes they exploited age-old tensions between France's farmers and city dwellers, the peasants' resentment of the urban rich, to convince them to risk selling their crops illegally on the black market rather than through government channels. And certainly the differences in profits were tempting. The French government-controlled markets could pay 3,000 francs for a cow, for instance, while a farmer could sell the same animal for 18,000 francs on the black market.

Establishing a legal, reliable market for food, then, was the biggest challenge facing the French in 1945. A report written by the new United Nations in March of that year found that many Europeans were trying to survive on a diet of 1,000 calories a day. (Between 2,000 and 2,500 a day is considered healthy, while the typical American will consume 5,000 calories at a single Thanksgiving meal.) The rate of malnutrition illnesses—like rickets, which bows the bones of children who don't have enough milk to drink—skyrocketed. The French tried to establish food priorities for returning "absents" and growing children. Even so, given the shortages, these allowances were paltry compared to what we enjoy today. Each French child from newborn to age three was guaranteed only one dried banana, for example, for the year of 1945. Food riots and demonstrations became common, such as the time 4,000 mothers marched on the Ministry of Supply at the Hôtel de Ville, shouting, "Milk for our little ones."

Faced with so many hurdles, political friction among the French started immediately. There was an uneasy alliance between predominantly communist and socialist Resistance fighters, or *maquis*, and General Charles de Gaulle, who headed the Free French army—soldiers who had escaped to England or North Africa when France fell to regroup and fight with the Allies. While their common goal was to liberate the nation, they coordinated their efforts well. Together, after D-day, they stabilized town and regional governments and controlled the purge, sending 40,000 collaborators to jail as opposed to their being killed on the street.

But the *maquis* and de Gaulle did not trust one another. De Gaulle often underplayed how important the Resistance had been during the war, and the *maquis* responded that they risked their lives in covert actions while he sat safely in London making plans. De Gaulle was more traditional and nationalistic in his thinking than the more radical *maquis*, who hoped to create a new social order as they rebuilt France. De Gaulle wanted a strong and independent France, a republic free of any outside political influences—America, Britain, or Soviet communism.

One way for de Gaulle to accomplish that was to create a sense of French pride and cohesiveness, a national myth—that France was united during the war and that the overwhelming majority of French bravely resisted the occupation. At Paris's liberation de Gaulle droned: "Paris broken! Paris martyrized! But Paris liberated! Liberated by itself, by its own people with the help of the armies of France, with the support and aid of France as a whole, of fighting France. . . ." Rarely did de Gaulle mention the Resistance or the Allies in his speeches, even as his soldiers paraded with tanks and trucks provided by the United States.

De Gaulle repeatedly pardoned collaborators that the *maquis*-controlled courts condemned; he commuted 73 percent of all death sentences. (He was not lenient on journalists or military officers, those who influenced others.) De Gaulle did this to push the country forward and to keep businesses running and local governments intact, operating with less offensive ex-Vichy bureaucrats. It also slowed the *maquis'* growing influence in the new government. He alienated many during "the Return" of the deportees by declaring: "The time for tears is over. The time for glory has returned." (It was not until 1954 that France established a day to commemorate the deported.) Although a war hero, de Gaulle's standing among the people was also marred by the horrendous food shortages and his failure to mention how he planned to provide them butter in his long speeches about "eternal France." Instead, the "battle for beef" was waged mostly by socialist reformers and committees of angry housewives. Ultimately, de Gaulle and the Resistance had difficulty governing together. As a result, de Gaulle withdrew from politics in 1946. But, in 1958, he returned to power, helping to reorganize France into its Fifth Republic, to end its war in Algiers, and to serve as its president until 1969, overseeing a decade of great economic growth for France.

The Cold War—the nuclear standoff between the Soviet Union and the United States—began the instant Germany collapsed. Stalin immediately absorbed Romania, Poland, and Czechoslovakia into the Soviet Communist bloc, behind his "iron curtain." His persecution of certain Eastern European ethnic groups was as bad as Hitler's. Stalin ruthlessly eliminated those who spoke out against his policies. The estimates of how many people died under his repressive regime—executed or sent to Gulag labor camps in Siberia—vary. But a conservative figure is 20 million.

Our understandable distrust of Stalin and his Soviet Union's brutal communism was so strong, the United States and Great Britain would secretly use notorious Gestapo like Klaus Barbie to spy on the Soviets because their intelligence gathering had been so precise during the war. Barbie had been headquartered in southern France, in Lyon, where Resistance groups were strong. Under his command, 7,500 people were deported, and 4,342 murdered. Barbie was so cruel in his interrogations and fanatical in his hunting of the *maquis* and Jews, the French called him "the butcher of Lyon." He was the officer who insisted on tracking down and executing the 44 Jewish children, aged four to 17, whom Sabine Zlatin had hidden in Izieu.

For ten years after the war, Barbie ran an anticommunist spy network for British and American intelligence communities in Germany and France. When the French realized he still lived and sought to arrest him, the U.S. Counter Intelligence Corps (CIC) helped him escape to Bolivia. In 1987, he was finally brought to trial and sentenced to life for crimes against humanity.

Yes, Madame Zlatin, the manager of the Lutetia's deportation center, existed. (She lived to testify against Barbie.) My portrayal of the Vercors's *le patron*, Father Gagnol, and "the bearded" priest are based on the real people. The Vercors *maquis*, desperate for trained soldiers, did liberate 52 Senegalese soldiers from a Nazi garrison, and risked a raid into Grenoble headquarters to steal plaster to set the broken arm of an SOE officer. The Vercors was crushed, their brave citizens "exterminated" in the gruesome manners described, and worse. One of the few prisoners the Nazis spared was the young OSS officer from South Carolina. They typically showed more mercy to Americans than to the French, whom Hitler hated.

Paris was indeed a hotbed of political excitement and

idealistic dreams following the war. New ways of governing were enthusiastically debated over pâté and brie in the cafés of the city's Saint Germain-de-Prés quarter. French philosophers and writers—Albert Camus, Jean-Paul Sartre, and Simone de Beauvoir—were daily regulars at the Café des Deux Magots and Café Flore. Parisians gathered to listen to them—especially Camus, whose underground newspaper, *Combat,* had been such an inspirational voice during the Resistance. Painter Pablo Picasso was also a large presence in Paris at the time, adding his voice to the French communist movement.

French women were granted the vote for the first time in 1944. As the country was liberated town by town, women often became mayors or other officials until the 1.5 million French POWs could be released and come home to govern. Activists like the fictional character Claudette, emboldened by their work in the Resistance, campaigned for new feminist laws and permanent seats in legislatures. In October 1945, 33 women were elected to the Constituent Assembly, which wrote France's new constitution. Called "the Glorious 33," nineteen had been in the Resistance, seven were arrested and imprisoned, and three survived Ravensbruck.

Well-known authors and war correspondents—like Ernest Hemingway and George Orwell—were in Paris as well, staying at the Hotel Scribe. Hemingway made an early entrance into the city during its fight for liberation, and gleefully joined in the roundups of what Nazis remained. George Orwell was in and out of Paris throughout the spring of 1945. He filed nineteen dispatches on the war for the *London Observer* and *Manchester Evening News*. He was definitely in town on VE day, and carried a Colt .32 that Hemingway gave him. Sadly, Orwell's wife had just died and would not see the publication of his groundbreaking satire of Stalin's collectivist farms—*Animal Farm*—in August 1945. Orwell died of tuberculosis five years later.

One thing Americans were reluctant to discuss following WWII was the emotional trauma many veterans faced. Back then readjustment issues we now know as symptoms of post-traumatic stress disorder (PTSD) were simply called "battle fatigue" or being "flak-happy." Often such troubles were dismissed as something veterans would get over with time and their return to normal, civilian life.

Coping was perhaps easier for WWII veterans than it would be later for Vietnam soldiers, who came home to war protests condemning their actions and who ended up suffering staggering rates of substance abuse, violence, and failed relationships. By comparison, WWII vets were hailed as heroes, the economy boomed, and they found jobs. Even so, the National Center for PTSD now estimates that one in twenty WWII vets suffered PTSD symptoms such as bad dreams, extreme irritability, and flashbacks. Those who did struggle with readjustment often masked their distress by becoming workaholics or drinking heavily at before-dinner cocktail hours—behaviors that were accepted norms during the 1950s and '60s.

Sadly, many of our surviving and elderly WWII veterans experience delayed onset of PTSD as their memory falters in general. Their ability to suppress disturbing images or flashbacks has eroded. Some are experiencing combat nightmares or violent reactions when awakened by spouses or caretakers. It is disturbing proof of how long lasting the impact of war is, that decades later, self-defense reflexes are still so ingrained in the subconscious of 80-year-old retirees.

The longer a person serves in combat situations, the more vulnerable he or she is to PTSD. In 2008, a Defense Department study found one in six soldiers and marines returning from Iraq suffered PTSD or depression. Many of these individuals had to serve multiple tours of duty.

PTSD symptoms include: nightmares and difficulty sleeping; flashbacks; memories intruding into present-day situations; hypervigilance, jumpiness, or persistent anxiety; sudden, overreactive rage or violence; feelings of profound guilt; and an inability to relate properly to others.

These are feelings and disturbances Henry combats as

he fights to negotiate his own internal peace.

Before writing this novel, I read memoirs by Resistance fighters, Ravensbruck prisoners, U.S. soldiers, American diplomats, and writers like Simone de Beauvoir and Marguerite Duras. I wept through many. Their pain and their phenomenal triumph of spirit cut clear through me. These journals also provided palpable day-to-day details—things like Paris's euphoric celebration of VE Day; the staggering price of eggs; being rationed to one hour of electricity a day; riots over strawberries and butter; people jailed for fighting over matches because replacement boxes could not be found; catchphrases such as "suitcase bearers" and "absents;" the lilacs dropped in puddles at the sight of returning deportees; the degradation of deportees being sprayed with DDT to remove lice; or the heartbreaking pleas of starved deportees to taste cherries.

Pamphlets like "112 Gripes about the French," issued in 1945 by the Information and Educational Division of the U.S. Occupational Forces, highlighted the era's lingo and misunderstandings between French civilians and American GIs. (Tragically, some deportees did die after our troops liberated concentration camps because, in pity and shock, GIs would hand whatever candy or K-rations they had in their pockets to the starving prisoners. Their stomachs were not ready for real food.)

Newspaper articles told of German POWs carving swastikas into peaches; Parisians wearing "lampshade" skirts fashioned from strips of any material they could find; elderly Frenchmen pulling out Jazz Age cigarette holders to smoke discarded butts down to their very last centimeter of nicotine; and the extraordinary efforts to evacuate and hide 400,000 Louvre treasures before Hitler marched into Paris. Photos taken by photojournalists like Lee Miller sparked scenes such as the girl selling milk from a dog-drawn cart, sweat-soaked men madly pedaling bicycles to generate electricity for hair dryers in Parisian salons; and children taking shelter in cardboard and bench teepees.

Two lines in the preface to the French edition of *Suite Française* spawned the time frame and many of the plot twists of this novel. *Suite Française* is a bestselling novel about the German occupation written by Irene Némirovsky, a well-known Jewish author of the time. She was deported and died in Auschwitz before she could finish. Her two young daughters managed to carry the manuscript with them as their governess and a succession of nuns willing to protect them moved them from one hiding place to the next. It was published 60 years later. The two lines had to do with the daughters standing at the Gare de l'Est holding name signs, hoping Irene or their father would be among the thousands of returning "absents" stumbling off those trains. That image of Némirovsky's children was haunting. Henry needed to find Pierre at that train station or the Hotel Lutetia.

That required the novel to take place between April and September 1945, while the Lutetia's center operated. Getting Henry into France in early 1945, not through the Air Force, was tricky. There was an outpouring of generosity from Americans in late 1945, as organizations (such as UNICEF) formed to ship over food, clothes, and livestock to replenish decimated farms. But they were just getting started in the spring of that year. I am grateful to Peggy Reiff Miller (www.seagoingcowboys.com) for sharing her research of "seagoing cowboys" and the boatloads of cows and horses organized by the Church of the Brethren and what became Heifer International. Trafford Doherty, director of New York's Glenn H. Curtiss Museum, helped clarify the mechanics of flying a Curtiss Jenny biplane. Macs Smith did quick, smart research into little-known organizations like the Union de Femmes Françaises, which helped pinpoint historic events to include.

My main thanks go to my family for their tremendous help with *A Troubled Peace*. My then 18-year-old daughter, Megan, traveled with me to Paris as my translator and coresearcher. In a whirlwind four days, we stayed at the Hotel Lutetia, visited war memorials and exhibits, and collected obscure writings about the return of the deportees. It took persistent digging, as information about that disturbing time is not readily advertised. She continued to translate websites and memoirs as I wrote. Without her fluent French and her astute, compassionate, and comprehensive questions, this novel would not be as complete a portrait as it is. My son, Peter, then 14, fielded constant hypothetical questions from me as I made choices regarding plot, themes, scenes, and characters. He is a wonderful first-read editor, insightful about history and people, a manuscript's pacing, and the clarity of its themes. Both he and his sister have a profound influence on my characters and the challenges I choose to hurl at them. And enduring thanks go to my husband, John, who has encouraged and advised me since college, patiently waiting through hundreds of deadlines and the emotional weight I carry when researching stories like this one. He reminds me of what truly matters in such stories and helps me find it in myself to write them.

Finally, to my editors: Katherine Tegen trusted that a magazine journalist could write a compelling novel. Her nurturing and shrewd sense of story brought about *Under a War-Torn Sky*, the precursor tale of Henry's survival behind the lines, and now *A Troubled Peace*. Thanks as well to Julie Lansky, who has added her deft editing strokes to Katherine's in guiding this novel. My long-time editor at the *Washingtonian* magazine, Jack Limpert, wisely told me that the two hardest and most important things to do in writing are to make people laugh and to make them cry; to be sure to include elements of both where possible; and to let the inherent ironies of day-to-day life speak for themselves.

Today, the Gare de l'Est still bustles. Its platforms are covered with vaulted glass ceilings supported by a lacy Art Deco latticework of green iron beams, creating a sense of airiness and light. The floor vibrates slightly as trains pull in and out. Short blasts of brakes and ringing bells signal arrivals and departures. Parisians and business travelers leaving the city for country and weekend holidays pass youths coming off the trains carrying overstuffed backpacks and excited expressions. They are greeted by the scent of just-out-of-the-oven rolls, warmed milk and coffee, and spring flowers in the booths along the tracks.

Only a few notice the four stone plaques on the floor by the exit, crowned with fresh wreaths of flowers and red, white, and blue banners. The plaques commemorate the POWs, the political deportees, the forced laborers, and the Jews who left France through Gare de l'Est "in a tragic voyage to prisons and torture camps and to death at the hands of the German Nazis." One honors the efforts of the railway workers to speed the return of those who somehow survived.

The handful of travelers who do notice these small memorials stop, café au lait or croissant in hand. A few look back to the trains behind them, perhaps imagining very different smells and sounds and voices. They draw in a deep breath or shake their heads before moving on, reminded of how lucky they are, and that thanks to the brave people who fought against such odds and such cruelty, we are free to enjoy and build a safe life the "absents" could only remember in their dreams.

Let us never forget their struggle toward the heights.

L. M. ELLIOTT is the author of several award-winning novels for young adults, including UNDER A WAR-TORN SKY, a Notable Children's Trade Book in the Field of Social Studies (NCSS/CBC) and a Jefferson Cup Honor Book, GIVE ME LIBERTY, and ANNIE, BETWEEN THE STATES, a New York Public Library Book for the Teen Age and an IRA/CBC Teachers' Choice. She lives with her husband and their two children in Virginia. You can visit the author online at www.lmelliott.com.